Notting Hill

Richard Curtis
Notting Hill

photographs by Clive Coote

with an afterword by Hugh Grant
line drawings by Trevor Flynn

Hodder & Stoughton

First published in 1999 by Hodder & Stoughton
A division of Hodder Headline PLC

British Library Cataloguing in Publication Data

ISBN 0 340 7344 8 (paperback)
0 340 73845 6 (hardback)
Typeset in Franklin Gothic and Adobe Garamond
Origination Trichrom
Printed and bound in Great Britain by Butler and Tanner

Design Studio Myerscough

Hodder & Stoughton
A division of Hodder Headline PLC
338 Euston Road
London
NW1 3BH

This book is dedicated to

Roger and **Duncan** who laboured with me over every scene, on the page, on the sound stage, and on the Lightworks.

Francesca who typed and tended to this script through draft after draft.

My sister **Belinda**, who looked after me.

Emma who read everything and improved everything

and

Scarlett and **Jake** who quite rightly ignored the whole damn process.

William

Honey

Anna

Bernie

Bella

Max

Spike

Martin

Contents

A Foreword

I suppose I started writing this film about thirty-four years ago. I was seven years old, and every night, to lull myself to sleep with a smile, I would have the same fantasy. It was my sister's birthday. Presents were unwrapped – and there didn't seem to be one from me. She would be unhappy, and then I'd say – 'Oh yes, well, actually, I did get you one little thing' – then walk to a big cupboard and swing the doors open – and there inside would be the four Beatles. They'd come out, chat, sing 'And I Love Her' – and leave. And then I'd be asleep.

Twenty-five years later, I was still having the same dream. The personnel had changed, but the basic plot was still the same. Now, when I couldn't get to sleep, I would imagine going to dinner with my friends Piers and Paula, in Battersea, as I did most weeks. I'd casually say I was bringing a girl – and then turn up unexpectedly with Madonna – usually Madonna, sometimes Isabella Rossellini – but usually Madonna. Piers would open the door, and be very cool about it, though secretly thrilled – his wife Paula would have no idea who Madonna was and behave accordingly – and my friend Helen would arrive late and explode with excitement. By which time, I'd have dozed off again.

Five years later, we were doing the first week's filming of 'Four Weddings' and I was sitting in a cold room in Luton Hoo, beside James Fleet, asleep, trying to work out what I should write next. I remembered these dreams, and thought it's not a bad idea for films to be about dreamy situations – and so I decided I'd have a bash at writing a film about someone very ordinary going out with someone very famous.

This script is the result of that.

And what we tried to do throughout the process was to make the dream realistic. The film is a concealed fairytale – the Princess & the Woodcutter as it were – but we tried to make it seem as though this sort of thing might actually happen – realistic direction, pretty realistic performances, not too slushy music. And by the end of writing the film, I think I'd started to believe it myself, that it was absolutely possible for just some guy to stay cool in the face of a huge star, and for things to work out. And I hoped that people who watched the film would, for an hour or two, believe the dream too.

But don't be taken in. This, to my shame, is the truth of it –

Not long ago, a friend of mine rang up at about eight one evening to say that she was actually having dinner with Madonna in Notting Hill and they might drop round for a drink after dinner. Would that be okay? My girlfriend said, 'Yes, fine, you know, either way, we're just in for the evening', hung up and we both calmly got back to work. You know, if she comes, she comes, no point fussing.

A few minutes later, Emma drifted upstairs. I took advantage of this just very quickly to check how stupid my hair was looking and squash it down a bit. Then I nipped back and started typing again.

I needn't have rushed, as I heard the sound of running water. Emma was washing her hair.

I quickly rushed round the house and took down the very uncool picture of myself with Madge from Neighbours. I also washed the dishes and put on a less small and baby-dribbled jumper.

Emma then emerged from the bathroom – and refused to concede that the hair thing had anything to do with Madonna. Her head had been itchy. How was my work going? 'Very well.'

PROD. THE NOTTING HILL FILM
ROLL 224 SLATE 406 TAKE 2
DIRECTOR ROGER M...
...MERA MICHAEL ...BSC
DAY
FILTER ...YNC

Domino's Pizza have been making delicious pizza for over 35 years using only fresh, never frozen dough.

While she dried her hair I quickly riffled through our record collection, and replaced the Neil Diamond CD that was playing with Crowded House. Then Van Morrison. Then Iris Dement. Then All Saints. Then Ron Sexsmith. Then I gave up and switched the music off altogether . . .

By the time Emma came downstairs she had changed completely. 'Why have you changed?' I asked. 'No reason.' 'Yes, actually, I'm a bit uncomfy too, I think I might change.'

Fifteen minutes later we were both wearing rather smart, though casual, suits. At which point I started to panic about my video collection. What the fuck would Madonna make of the fact I had a copy of 'Four Weddings' in Japanese in quite a prominent position? And two copies of 'Bean'. And a copy of 'Body of Evidence'. It took about twenty-five minutes to sort everything out. French films galore shot into prime position, though not ones I might just have bought because Emmanuelle Beart is naked in them.

Meanwhile Emma redecorated the entire house. Carpets disappeared. Rather stylish black and white photographs, long since replaced by drawings done by my daughter, found themselves back on the walls. The downstairs bathroom radiator was turned on for the first time in a year – the door into the unattractive laundry room closed for the first time ever – and the couches subtly shifted so it didn't look as though we spend our whole fucking boring lives just watching television.

Then we set back to work. For about five minutes, when I gave in and washed my hair and Emma changed out of the suit into a cashmere jumper and woke up my son and put him into cute little pyjamas instead of a hideous one-piece with a lot of naff cats on it.

We'd just finished this – and cleaning the kitchen – when the bell rang. It was a courier with a script Emma needed for the next day. I nearly strangled him.

After which we settled down once and for all, both typing – wouldn't it be kind of cool and conscientious to be found working, just, you know, calmly working, not having lifted a single finger to prepare for the arrival of this fabulous iconic creature, who just begged her papa not to preach.

We worked on till one o'clock in the morning, when we went to sleep, very clean, very relieved, and very ashamed of the big lie that is the film you're about to read.

Richard Curtis, Spring 1999

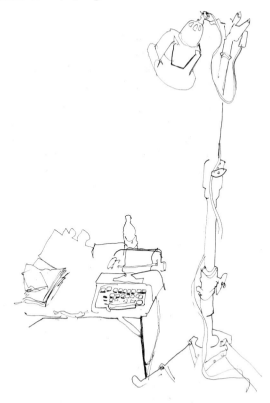

may be the face I can't forget

titles.

1. **ext. Various Days.**

'She' plays through the credits.'

Exquisite footage of Anna Scott – the great movie star of our time – an ideal – the perfect star and woman – her life full of glamour and sophistication and mystery.

2. **ext. Street. Day.**

Mix through to William, 35, relaxed, pleasant, informal. We follow him as he walks down Portobello Road, carrying a loaf of bread. It is spring.

William (v/o) Of course, I've seen her films and always thought she was, well, fabulous – but, you know, a million, million miles from from the world I live in. Which is here – Notting Hill – not a bad place to be . . .

3. **ext. Portobello Road. Day.**

It's a full fruit market day.

William (v/o) There's the market on weekdays, selling every fruit and vegetable known to man . . .

4. **ext. Portobello Road. Day.**

A man in denims exits the tattoo studio.

William (v/o) The tattoo parlour – with a guy outside who got drunk and now can't remember why he chose 'I Love Ken'. . .

5. **ext. Portobello Road. Day.**

William (v/o) The radical hair-dressers where everyone comes out looking like the Cookie Monster, whether they like it or not . . .

Sure enough, a girl exits with a huge threaded blue bouffant.

6. **ext. Portobello Road. Saturday.**

William (v/o)   Then suddenly it's the weekend, and from break of day, hundreds of stalls appear out of nowhere, filling Portobello Road right up to Notting Hill Gate . . .

A frantic crowded Portobello market.

. . . and thousands of people buy millions of antiques, some genuine . . .

The camera finally settles on a stall selling beautiful stained glass windows of various sizes, some featuring biblical scenes and saints.

. . . and some not so genuine.

The final stained glass window is in the same style – but the featured saints are Beavis and Butthead.

7. **ext. Golborne Road. Day.**

William (v/o)   And what's great is that lots of friends have ended up in this part of London – that's Tony, architect turned chef, who recently invested all the money he ever earned in a new restaurant . . .

Shot of Tony proudly setting out a board outside his restaurant, the sign still being painted. He receives and approves a huge fresh salmon.

8. **ext. Portobello Road. Day.**

William   So this is where I spend my days and years – in this small village in the middle of a city – in a house with a blue door that my wife and I bought together . . . before she left me for a man who looked like Harrison Ford, only even handsomer . . .

We arrive outside his blue-doored house just off Portobello.

. . . and where I now lead a strange half-life with a lodger called . . .

WREATHS · CROSSES · OASIS · BOU
bu order tel :- 221 332

9.   int. William's House. Day.

William   Spike!

*The house has far too many things in it. Definitely a
two-bachelor flat.*

*Spike appears. An unusual looking fellow. He has unusual
hair, unusual facial hair and an unusual Welsh accent:
very white, as though his flesh has never seen the sun.
He wears only shorts.*

Spike   Even he. Hey, you couldn't help me with an incredibly
important decision, could you?

William   This is important in comparison to, let's say, whether
they should cancel third world debt?

Spike   That's right – I'm at last going out on a date with the
great Janine and I just want to be sure I've picked the
right t-shirt.

William   What are the choices?

Spike   Well . . . wait for it . . .

He pulls on a t-shirt . . .

First there's this one . . .

*The t-shirt is white with a horrible looking plastic alien
coming out of it, jaws open, blood everywhere.
It says 'I Love Blood'.*

Cool, huh?

William   Yes – might make it hard to strike a really
romantic note.

Spike   Point taken.

He heads back up the stairs . . . talks as he changes . . .

I suspect you'll prefer the next one.

*And he re-enters in a white t-shirt, with a large arrow,
pointing down to his flies, saying, 'Get It Here'.*

William Yes – she might think you don't have true love on your mind.

Spike Wouldn't want that . . . *(and back up he goes)* Okay – just one more.

He comes down wearing it. Lots of hearts, saying, 'You're the most beautiful woman in the world'.

William Well, yes, that's perfect. Well done.

Spike Thanks. Great. Wish me luck.

William Good luck.

Spike turns and walks upstairs proudly. Revealing that on the back of the t-shirt, also printed in big letters, is written 'Fancy a fuck?'

10.   **ext. Portobello Road. Day.**

William (v/o)   And so it was just another hopeless Wednesday, as
I set off through the market to work, little suspecting that
this was the day which would change my life forever. This is
work, by the way, my little travel book shop . . .

*A small unpretentious store . . . named 'The Travel
Book Co.'*

. . . which, well, sells travel books – and, to be frank
with you, doesn't always sell many of those.

William enters.

11. **int. The Bookshop. Day.**

It is a small shop, slightly chaotic, bookshelves everywhere, with little secret bits round corners with even more books. Martin, William's sole employee, is waiting enthusiastically. He is very keen, an uncrushable optimist. Perhaps without cause. A few seconds later, William stands gloomily behind the desk.

William Classic. Absolutely classic. Profit from major sales push – minus £347.

Martin Shall I go get a cappuccino? Ease the pain.

William Yes, better get me a half. All I can afford.

Martin I get your logic. Demi-capu coming up.

He salutes and bolts out the door – as he does, a woman walks in. We only just glimpse her.

Cut to William working. He looks up casually. And sees something. His reaction is hard to read. After a pause . . .

William	Can I help you?
	It is Anna Scott, the biggest movie star in the world – here – in his shop. The most divine, subtle, beautiful woman on earth. When she speaks she is very self-assured and self-contained.
Anna	No, thanks. I'll just look around.
William	Fine.
	She wanders over to a shelf as he watches her – and picks out a quite smart coffee table book.
William	That book's really not good – just in case, you know, browsing turned to buying. You'd be wasting your money.
Anna	Really?
William	Yes. This one though is . . . very good.

He picks up a book on the counter.

I think the man who wrote it has actually been to Turkey, which helps. There's also a very amusing incident with a kebab.

Anna   Thanks. I'll think about it.

William suddenly spies something odd on the small TV monitor beside him.

William   If you could just give me a second.

Her eyes follow him as he moves towards the back of the shop and approaches a man in slightly ill-fitting clothes.

William   Excuse me.

Thief   Yes.

William   Bad news.

Thief	What?
William	We've got a security camera in this bit of the shop.
Thief	So?
William	So, I saw you put that book down your trousers.
Thief	What book?
William	The one down your trousers.
Thief	I haven't got a book down my trousers.
William	Right – well, then we have something of an impasse. I tell you what – I'll call the police – and, what can I say? – if I'm wrong about the whole book-down-the-trousers scenario, I really apologise.
Thief	Okay – what if I did have a book down my trousers?

William	Well, ideally, when I went back to the desk, you'd remove the Cadogan guide to Bali from your trousers, and either wipe it and put it back, or buy it. See you in a sec.
	He returns to his desk. In the monitor we just glimpse, as does William, the book coming out of the trousers and put back on the shelves. The thief drifts out towards the door. Anna, who has observed all this, is looking at a blue book on the counter.
William	Sorry about that . . .
Anna	No, that's fine. I was going to steal one myself but now I've changed my mind. Signed by the author, I see.
William	Yes, we couldn't stop him. If you can find an unsigned copy, it's worth an absolute fortune.
	She smiles. Suddenly the thief is there.
Thief	Excuse me.

Anna	Yes.
Thief	Can I have your autograph?
Anna	What's your name?
Thief	Rufus.
	She signs his scruffy piece of paper. He tries to read it.
	What does it say?
Anna	Well, that's the signature – and above, it says 'Dear Rufus – you belong in jail'.

Thief	Nice one. Would you like my phone number?
Anna	Tempting but . . . no, thank you.

Thief leaves.

I think I will try this one.

She hands William a £20 note and the book he said was rubbish. He talks as he handles the transaction.

William	Oh – right – on second thoughts maybe it wasn't that bad. Actually – it's a sort of masterpiece really. None of those childish kebab stories you get in so many travel books these days. And I'll throw in one of these for free.

He drops in one of the signed books.

Very useful for lighting fires, wrapping fish, that sort of thing.

She looks at him with a slight smile.

Anna	Thanks.

And leaves. She's out of his life forever. William is a little dazed. Seconds later Martin comes back in.

Martin	Cappuccino as ordered.
William	Thanks. I don't think you'll believe who was just in here.
Martin	Who? Someone famous?

But William's innate natural English discretion takes over.

William	No. No-one – no-one.

They set about drinking their coffees.

Martin	Would be exciting if someone famous did come into the shop though, wouldn't it? Do you know – this is pretty incredible actually – I once saw Ringo Starr. Or at least I think it was Ringo. It might have been that bloke from 'Fiddler On The Roof'. Toppy.
William	Topol.
Martin	That's right – Topol.

William	But Ringo Starr doesn't look anything like Topol.
Martin	No, well . . . he was quite a long way away.
William	So it could have been neither of them?
Martin	I suppose so.
William	Right. It's not a classic anecdote, is it?
Martin	Not classic, no.

Martin shakes his head. William drains his cappuccino.

William	Right – want another one?
Martin	Yes. No, wait – let's go crazy – I'll have an orange juice.

12. **ext. Portobello Road. Day.**

William sets off.

13. **int. Coffee Shop. Day.**

William collects his juice in a coffee shop on Westbourne Park Road.

14.   ext. Portobello Road. Day.

William swings out of the little shop – he turns the
corner of Portobello Road and bumps straight into Anna.
The orange juice, in its foam cup, flies. It soaks Anna.

Anna   Oh Jesus.

William   Here, let me help.

He grabs some paper napkins and starts to clean it off
– getting far too near her breasts in the panic of it . . .

Anna   What are you doing?!

He jumps back.

William   Nothing, nothing . . . Look, I live just over the street
– you could get cleaned up.

Anna   No thank you. I need to get my car back.

William   I also have a phone. I'm confident that in five minutes we can have you spick and span and back on the street again . . . in the non-prostitute sense obviously.

In his diffident way, he is confident, despite her being genuinely annoyed. She turns and looks at him.

Anna   Okay. So what does 'just over the street' mean – give it to me in yards.

William   Eighteen yards. That's my house there.

He doesn't lie – it is eighteen yards away. She looks down. She looks up at him.

15.   **int. William's House. Corridor. Day.**

They enter. She carries a few stylish bags.

William   Come on in. I'll just . . .

William runs in further – it's a mess. He kicks some old shoes under the stairs, bins an unfinished pizza and hides a plate of breakfast in a cupboard. She enters the kitchen.

It's not that tidy, I fear.

And he guides her up the stairs, after taking the bag of books from her . . .

The bathroom is right at the top of the stairs and there's a phone on the desk up there.

She heads upstairs.

16.   **int. Kitchen. Day.**

William is tidying up frantically. Then he hears Anna's feet on the stairs. She walks down, wearing a short, sparkling black top beneath her leather jacket. With her trainers still on. He is dazzled by the sight of her.

William   Would you like a cup of tea before you go?

Anna   No thanks.

William   Coffee?

Anna   No.

William   Orange juice – probably not.

He moves to his very empty fridge – and offers its only contents.

Something else cold – coke, water, some disgusting sugary drink pretending to have something to do with fruits of the forest?

Anna   Really, no.

William   Would you like something to nibble – apricots, soaked in honey – quite why, no-one knows – because it stops them tasting of apricots, and makes them taste like honey, and if you wanted honey, you'd just buy honey, instead of apricots, but nevertheless – there we go – yours if you want them.

Anna   No.

William   Do you always say 'no' to everything?

Pause. She looks at him deep.

Anna   No. *(pause)* I better be going. Thanks for your help.

William   You're welcome and, may I also say . . . heavenly.

It has taken a lot to get this out loud. He is not a smooth-talking man.

Take my one chance to say it. After you've read that terrible book, you're certainly not going to be coming back to the shop.

She smiles. She's cool.

Anna	Thank you.
William	Yes. Well. My pleasure.

He guides her towards the door.

Nice to meet you. Surreal but nice.

In a slightly awkward movement, he shows her out the door. He closes the door and shakes his head in wonder. Then . . .

'Surreal but nice'. What was I thinking?

. . . He shakes his head again in horror and wanders back along the corridor in silence. There's a knock on the door. He moves back, casually . . .

Coming.

He opens the door. It's her.

Oh hi. Forget something?

Anna	I forgot my bag.
William	Oh right.

He shoots into the kitchen and picks up the forgotten shopping bag. Then returns and hands it to her.

Here we go.

Anna	Thanks. Well . . .

They stand in that corridor – in that small space. Second time saying goodbye. A strange feeling of intimacy. She leans forward and she kisses him. Total silence. A real sense of the strangeness of those lips, those famous lips on his. They part.

William	I apologise for the 'surreal but nice' comment. Disaster . . .
Anna	Don't worry about it. I thought the apricot and honey business was the real lowpoint.

Suddenly there is a clicking of a key in the lock.

William	Oh my God. My flatmate. I'm sorry – there's no excuse for him.

Spike walks in . . .

Spike   Hi.

Anna   Hi.

William   Hi.

Spike walks past unsuspiciously and heads into the kitchen.

Spike   I'm just going to go into the kitchen to get some food – and then I'm going to tell you a story that will make your balls shrink to the size of raisins.

And leaves them in the corridor.

Anna   Probably best not tell anyone about this.

William   Right. No-one. I mean, I'll tell myself sometimes but . . . don't worry – I won't believe it.

Anna   Bye.

And she leaves, with just a touch of William's hand. Spike comes out of the kitchen, eating something white out of a styrofoam container with a spoon.

Spike　There's something wrong with this yogurt.

William　It's not yogurt – it's mayonnaise.

Spike　Well, there you go. *(takes another big spoonful)* On for a video fest tonight? I've got some absolute classics.

17.　int. William's Living Room. Night.

The lights are off. William and Spike on the couch, just the light from the TV playing on their faces. Cut to the TV full screen. There is Anna. She is in a stylish Woody Allen type modern romantic comedy, 'Gramercy Park', in black and white.

18.　int. Manhattan Art Gallery. Day.

Anna's character – Woody Anna – is walking around the gallery with her famous co-star, Michael. They should be the perfect couple, but there is tension. Anna is not happy.

Michael　Smile.

Anna　No.

Michael　Smile.

Anna　I've got nothing to smile about.

Michael　Okay in about 7 seconds, I'm going to ask you to marry me.

And after a couple of seconds – wow – she smiles.

19.　int. William's Living Room. Night.

Spike　Imagine – somewhere in the world there's a man who's allowed to kiss her.

William　Yes, she is fairly fabulous.

20. **int. Bookshop. Day.**

The next day. William and Martin quietly co-existing.
An annoying customer enters. Mr Smith.

Mr Smith   Do you have any books by Dickens?

William   No, we're a travel bookshop. We only sell travel books.

Mr Smith   Oh right. How about that new John Grisham thriller?

William   No, that's a novel too.

Mr Smith   Oh right. Have you got a copy of 'Winnie the Pooh'?

Pause

William   Martin – your customer.

Martin   Can I help you?

William looks up. At that moment the entire window is
suddenly taken up by the huge side of a bus, obscuring the
light – and entirely covered with a portrait of Anna –
from her new film, 'Helix'.

21. **int. William's House. Corridor/Living Room. Day.**

William heads upstairs and passes Spike coming down,
wearing full body scuba diving gear.

Spike   Hey.

William   Hi . . .

21ᵃ. **int. William's Kitchen. Day.**

The two of them fixing a cup of tea in the kitchen.

William   Just incidentally – why are you wearing that?

Spike   Ahm – combination of factors really. No
clean clothes . . .

William   There never will be, you know, unless you actually
clean your clothes.

Spike   Right. Vicious circle. And then I was like rooting
around in your things, and found this, and I thought –
cool. Kind of spacey.

22. **ext. William's Terrace. Day.**

The two of them on the rooftop terrace, passing the day.
William is reading 'The Bookseller'. The terrace is small
and the plants aren't great – but it overlooks London in a
rather wonderful way. Spike still in scuba gear, goggles on.

Spike	There's something wrong with the goggles though . . .
William	No, they were prescription, so I could see all the fishes properly.
Spike	Groovy. You should do more of this stuff.
William	So – any messages?
Spike	Yeh, I wrote a couple down.
William	Two? That's it?
Spike	You want me to write down all your messages?

William closes his eyes in exasperation.

William	Who were the ones you didn't write down from?
Spike	Ahm let's see – ahm. No. Gone completely. Oh no, wait. There was – one from your mum: she said don't forget lunch and her leg's hurting again.
William	Right. No-one else?
Spike	Absolutely not.

Spike leans back and relaxes.

Though if we're going for this obsessive writing-down-all-messages thing – some American girl called Anna called a few days ago.

William freezes – then looks at Spike.

William	What did she say?
Spike	Well, it was genuinely bizarre . . . she said, hi – it's Anna – and then she said, call me at the Ritz – and then gave herself a completely different name.
William	Which was?
Spike	Absolutely no idea. Remembering one name's bad enough . . .

23. **int. William's Living Room. Day.**

William on the phone. We hear the formal man at the other end of the phone. And then intercut with him.

William Hello.

Ritz man (v/o) May I help you, sir?

William Ahm, look this is a very odd situation. I'm a friend of Anna Scott's – and she rang me at home the day before yesterday – and left a message saying that she's staying with you . . .

24. **int. Ritz Reception. Day.**

Ritz man I'm sorry, we don't have anyone of that name here, sir.

William No, that's right – I know that. She said she's using another name – but the problem is she left the message with my flatmate, which was a serious mistake.

25. **int. William's Living Room. Day.**

William (cont'd) Imagine if you will the stupidest person you've ever met – are you doing that . . . ?

Spike happens to be in the foreground of this shot. He's reading a newspaper.

Ritz man Yes, sir. I have him in my mind.

William And then double it – and that is the – what can I say – git I'm living with and he cannot remember . . .

Spike Try 'Flintstone'.

William (to Spike) What?

Spike I think she said her name was 'Flintstone'.

William Does 'Flintstone' mean anything to you?

Ritz man I'll put you right through, sir.

Flintstone is indeed the magic word.

William Oh my God.

He practises how to sound.

Hello. Hi. Hi.

Anna (v/o) Hi.

We hear her voice – don't see her.

William *(caught out)* Oh hi. It's William Thacker. We, ahm I work in a bookshop.

Anna (v/o) You played it pretty cool here, waiting for three days to call.

William No, I've never played anything cool in my entire life. Spike, who I'll stab to death later, never gave me the message.

Anna (v/o) Oh – Okay.

William Perhaps I could drop round for tea or something?

Anna (v/o) Yeh – unfortunately, things are going to be pretty busy, but . . . okay, let's give it a try. Four o'clock could be good.

William Right. Great. *(he hangs up)* Classic. Classic.

26. **ext. Ritz. Day.**

William jumps off a bus and walks towards the Ritz. He carries a small bunch of roses.

27. **int. Ritz Lobby. Day.**

He approaches the lifts. At the lift, he pushes the button and the doors open. As he is getting in, William is joined by a young man. His name is Tarquin.

William Which floor?

Tarquin Three.

William pushes the button. They wait for the doors to close.

28. **int. Ritz Corridor. Day.**

The lift lands. William gets out. So does Tarquin. Rooms 30-35 are to the left. 35-39 to the right. William heads right. So does Tarquin.

William is puzzled. He slows down as he approaches room 38. So does Tarquin. William stops, so does Tarquin. William points at the number.

William   Are you sure you . . . ?

Tarquin   Yes.

William   Oh. Right.

He knocks. A bright, well-tailored American girl opens the door.

Karen   Hello, I'm Karen. Sorry – things are running a bit late. Here's the thing . . .

She hands them a very slick, expensively produced press kit, with the poster picture of Anna, for the film 'Helix'.

29. **int. The Trafalgar Suite Ante-Room. Day.**

A few seconds later – they enter the main waiting room. There are a number of journalists waiting for their audience.

Karen   What did you think of the film?

Tarquin   Marvellous. 'Close Encounters' meets 'Jean De Florette'. Oscar-winning stuff.

They both turn to William for his opinion.

William   I agree.

Karen   I'm sorry. I didn't get down what magazines you're from.

Tarquin   'Time Out'.

Karen   Great. And you . . .

William   (seeing it on a coffee table) 'Horse and Hound'. The name's William Thacker. I think she might be expecting me.

Karen	Okay – take a seat. I'll check.
	They sit down as Karen goes off.
Tarquin	You've brought her flowers?
	William goes for the cover-up.
William	No – they're . . . for my grandmother. She's in a hospital nearby. Thought I'd kill two birds with one stone.
Tarquin	I'm sorry. Which hospital?
	Pause. He's in trouble.
William	Do you mind me not saying – it's a rather distressing disease and the name of the hospital rather gives it away.
Tarquin	Oh sure. Of course.
Karen	Mr Thacker.
	Saved by the bell.

30. int. Trafalgar Suite Corridor. Day.

Karen	You've got five minutes.
	He is shown in through big golden doors. Karen stays outside.

31. int. The Trafalgar Suite Sitting Room. Day.

	There Anna is, framed in the window. Glorious.
William	Hi.
Anna	Hello.
William	I brought these, but clearly . . .
	There are lots of other flowers in the room.
Anna	Oh no, no – these are great.
	A fair amount of tension. These two people hardly know each other – and the first and last time they met, they kissed.

William   Sorry about not ringing back. The whole two-names concept was totally too much for my flatmate's pea-sized intellect.

Anna   No, it's a stupid privacy thing. I always choose a cartoon character – last time out, I was Mrs Bambi.

At which moment Jeremy, Karen's boss, comes in. A fairly grave, authoritative fifty-year-old PR man consulting a list.

Jeremy   Everything okay?

Anna   Yes, thanks.

Jeremy   And you are from 'Horse and Hound' magazine?

William nods.

Anna   Is that so?

William shrugs his shoulders. Jeremy settles at a little desk in the corner and makes notes. A pause. William feels he has to act the part. They sit in chairs opposite each other.

William   So I'll just fire away shall I?

Anna nods.

Right. Ahm . . . the film's great . . . and I just wondered – whether you ever thought of having more . . . horses in it?

Anna   Ahm – well – we would have liked to – but it was difficult, obviously, being set in space.

William   Obviously. Very difficult.

Jeremy leaves.

William puts his head in his hands. He was pathetic.

I'm sorry – I arrived outside – they thrust this thing into my hand – I didn't know what to do.

Anna No, it's my fault, I thought this would all be over by now. I just wanted to sort of apologise for the kissing thing. I seriously don't know what got in to me. I just wanted to make sure you were fine about it.

William Absolutely fine about it.

Re-enter Jeremy.

Jeremy Do remember that Miss Scott is also keen to talk about her next project, which is shooting later in the summer.

William Oh yes – excellent. Ahm – any horses in that one? Or hounds, of course. Our readers are equally intrigued by both species.

Anna It takes place on a submarine.

William Yes. Right . . . But if there were horses, would you be riding them yourself or would you be getting a stunt horse person double sort of thing?

Jeremy exits.

I'm just a complete moron. Sorry. This is the sort of thing that happens in dreams – not in real life. Good dreams, obviously – it's a dream to see you.

Anna And what happens next in the dream?

It's a challenge.

William Well, I suppose in the dream dream scenario, I just . . . ahm, change my personality, because you can do that in dreams, and walk across and kiss the girl but you know it'll never happen.

Pause. Then they move towards each other when . . . Jeremy enters.

Jeremy Time's up, I'm afraid. Sorry it was so short. Did you get what you wanted?

William Very nearly.

Jeremy Maybe time for one last question?

William Right.

Jeremy goes out – it's their last seconds.

Are you busy tonight?

Anna Yes.

They look at each other. Jeremy enters, with another journalist in tow. Anna and William stand and shake hands formally.

Well, it was nice to meet you. Surreal but nice.

William Thank you. You are 'Horse and Hound's' favourite actress. You and Black Beauty. Tied.

32. int. Trafalgar Suite Corridor. Day.

William exits fairly despondent and heads for the door. Tarquin is in the corridor calling on his mobile phone.

Tarquin How was she?

William Fabulous.

Tarquin Wait a minute – she took your grandmother's flowers?

William can't think his way out of this.

William Yes. That's right. Bitch.

He turns to go, but is accosted by Karen.

Karen If you'd like to come with me we can rush you through the others.

William The others?

33. int. Ritz Interview Room. Day.

Karen Mr Thacker's from 'Horse and Hound'.

A forty-year-old actor with great presence warmly shakes William's hand.

Male lead Pleased to meet you. Did you like the film?

William Ah . . . yes, enormously.

Male lead Well, fire away.

William Right, right. Ahm – did you enjoy making the film?

Male lead   I did.

William   Any bit in particular?

Male lead   Well, you tell me which bit you liked most – and I'll tell you if I enjoyed making it.

William   Ahm right, right. I liked the bit in space very much. Did you enjoy making that bit?

34.   int. Ritz Interview Room. Day.

Same room, same seat, minutes later, with a monolingual foreign actor and an interpreter.

William   Did you identify with the character you were playing?

Interpreter   Te identificaste con el personaje que interpretabas?

Foreign actor   No.

Interpreter   No.

William   Ah. Why not?

Interpreter   Por que no?

Foreign actor   Porque es un robot carnivoro psicopata.

Interpreter   Because he is playing a psychopathic flesh-eating robot.

William   Classic.

35.   int. Ritz Interview Room. Day.

And now William is sitting opposite an eleven-year-old American girl.

William   Is this your first film?

Girl   No – it's my 22nd.

William   Of course it is. Any favourites among the 22?

Girl   Working with Leonardo.

William   Da Vinci?

Girl   Di Caprio.

William   Of course. And is he your favourite Italian film director?

36.   int. Ritz Corridor. Day.

William emerges traumatised into the corridor. It is full of camera crews. And there is Karen.

Karen   Mr Thacker.

William   *(so weary)* Yes?

Karen   Have you got a moment?

37.   int. Anna's Suite Sitting Room. Day.

They knock on her door.

Anna (v/o)   Come in.

William enters. A certain nervousness. They are alone again.

Anna   Ahm. That thing I was doing tonight – I'm not doing it any more. I told them I had to spend the evening with Britain's premier equestrian journalist.

William   Oh well, great. Perfect. Oh no – shittity brickitty – it's my sister's birthday – shit – we're meant to be having dinner.

Anna   Okay – fine.

William   But no, I'm sure I can get out of it.

Anna   No, I mean, if it's fine with you, I'll, you know, be your date.

William   You'll be my date at my little sister's birthday party?

Anna   If that's all right.

William   I'm sure it's all right. My friend Max is cooking and he's acknowledged to be the worst cook in the world, but, you know, you could hide the food in your hand-bag or something.

Anna   Okay.

William   Okay.

38. **int. Max and Bella's Kitchen/Living Room. Night.**

Bella and Max are in the kitchen.

Max He's bringing a girl?

Bella Miracles do happen.

Max Does the girl have a name?

Bella He wouldn't say.

Max Christ, what is going on in there?

The oven seems to be smoking a little. Then the bell rings.

(cont'd) Oh God.

It's bad timing. Max shoots out of the kitchen.

39. **int. Max and Bella's Corridor. Night.**

Max heads for the door impatiently. He opens it and turns back without looking at William and Anna standing there.

Max Come on in. Vague food crisis.

William and Anna move along the corridor to the kitchen.

40. **int. Max and Bella's Kitchen/Living Room. Night.**

Bella is there.

Bella Hiya – sorry – the guinea fowl is proving more complicated than expected.

William He's cooking guinea fowl?

Bella Don't even ask.

Anna Hi.

Bella Hi. Good Lord – you're the spitting image of . . .

William Bella – this is Anna.

Bella Right. *(pause)*

Max Okay. Crisis over.

He rises from his stove position.

William Max. This is Anna.

Max	Hello, Anna ahm . . . *(he recognises her — the word just falls out)* Scott – have some wine.
Anna	Thank you.

Door bell goes.

41.   int. Max and Bella's Corridor. Night.

Max opens the door – it is Honey.

Max	Hi.

She does a little pose, having worn a real party dress.

Yes, Happy Birthday.

They head back along the corridor.

Look, your brother has brought this girl, and ahm . . .

42.   int. Max and Bella's Kitchen/Living Room. Night.

They enter the kitchen.

Honey	Hi guys. *(sees Anna)* Oh holy fuck.
William	Hun – this is Anna. Anna – this is Honey – she's my baby sister.
Anna	Hiya.
Honey	Oh God this is one of those key moments in life, when it's possible you can be really, genuinely cool – and I'm going to fail a hundred percent. I absolutely and totally and utterly adore you and I think you're the most beautiful woman in the world and more importantly I genuinely believe and have believed for some time now that we can be best friends. What do you think?
Anna	Ahm . . . I think that sounds – you know – lucky me. Happy Birthday.

She hands her a present.

Honey	Oh my God. You gave me a present. We're best friends already. Marry Will – he's a really nice guy and then we can be sisters.
Anna	I'll think about it.

The front door bell goes.

Max   That'll be Bernie.

He heads out into the corridor to the front door.

43.   int. Max and Bella's Corridor. Night.

Max opens the door.

Max   Hello, Berns.

Bernie   I'm sorry I'm so late. Bollocksed up at work again, I fear. Millions down the drain.

44.   int. Max and Bella's Kitchen/Living Room. Night.

They enter the room.

Max   Bernie – this is Anna.

Bernie   Hello, Anna. Delighted to meet you.

Doesn't recognise her – turns to Honey.

Honey Bunny – happy birthday to you. *(hands her a present)* It's a hat. You don't have to wear it or anything.

45.   int. Max and Bella's Kitchen/Living Room. Night.

A minute or two later – they are standing, drinking wine before dinner. Bernie with Anna on their own – William helping Max in the kitchen.

Max   You haven't slept with her, have you?

William   That is a cheap question and the answer is, of course, no comment.

Max   'No comment' means 'yes'.

William   No, it doesn't.

Max   Do you ever masturbate?

William   Definitely no comment.

Max   You see – it means 'yes'.

Then on to Bernie's conversation.

Bernie   So tell me Anna – what do you do?

Anna	I'm an actress.
Bernie	Splendid. I'm actually in the stock-market, so not really similar fields, though I have done some amateur stuff – P. G. Wodehouse, you know – farce, all that. 'Ooh – careful there, vicar.' Always imagined it's a pretty tough job, though, acting. I mean the wages are a scandal, aren't they?
Anna	Well, they can be.
Bernie	I see friends from university – clever chaps – been in the business longer than you – they're scraping by on seven, eight thousand a year. It's no life. What sort of acting do you do?
Anna	Films mainly.
Bernie	Oh splendid. Well done. How's the pay in movies? I mean, last film you did, what did you get paid?
Anna	Fifteen million dollars.
Bernie	Right. Right. So that's . . . fairly good. On the high side . . . have you tried the nuts?
Max	Right – I think we're ready.

They all move towards the kitchen.

Anna	*(to Bella)* I wonder if you could tell me where the . . . ?
Bella	Oh, it's just down the corridor on the right.
Honey	I'll show you.

A moment's silence as they leave – then in a split second the others all turn to William.

Bella	Quickly, quickly – talk very quickly what are you doing here with Anna Scott?
Bernie	Anna Scott?
Bella	Yes.
Bernie	The movie star?
Bella	Yup.
Bernie	Oh God. Oh God. Oh Goddy God.

The horror of his remembered conversation slowly unfolds.
Honey re-enters.

Honey I don't believe it. I walked into the loo with her. I was still talking when she started unbuttoning her jeans . . . She had to ask me to leave.

46. **int. Max and Bella's Conservatory. Night**.

A little later. They are sat at dinner. Bella next to Anna.

Bella What do you think of the guinea fowl?

Anna *(whispering)* I'm a vegetarian.

Bella Oh God.

47. **int. Max and Bella's Conservatory. Night.**

Moving on through the evening – they are very relaxed, as they eat dinner. A few seconds watching the evening going well – Anna is taking this in – real friends – relaxed – easy, teasing. And there's a cake. Honey wears Bernie's unsuitable hat. Anna watches William laughing at something and then putting his head in his hands with mock shame.

48. **int. Max and Bella's Conservatory. Night.**

Coffee time.

Max Having you here, Anna, firmly establishes what I've long suspected, that we really are the most desperate lot of under-achievers.

Bernie Shame!

Max I'm not saying it's a bad thing. In fact, I think it's something we should take pride in. I'm going to give the last brownie as a prize to the saddest act here.

A little pause. Then William turns to Bernie.

William Bernie.

Bernie   Well, obviously it's me, isn't it – I work in the City
in a job I don't understand and everyone keeps getting
promoted above me. I haven't had a girlfriend since . . .
puberty and, well, the long and short of it is, nobody
fancies me, and if these cheeks get any chubbier,
they never will.

Honey   Nonsense. I fancy you. Or I did before you got so fat.

Max   You see – and unless I'm much mistaken, your job still
pays you rather a lot of money, while Honey here, she
earns nothing flogging her guts out at London's seediest
record store.

Honey   Yes. And I don't have hair – I've got feathers, and I've
got funny goggly eyes, and I'm attracted to cruel men
and . . . no-one'll ever marry me because my boosies
have actually started shrinking.

Max   You see – incredibly sad.

Bella   On the other hand, her best friend is Anna Scott.

Honey   That's true, I can't deny it. She needs me, what
can I say?

Bella   And most of her limbs work. Whereas I'm stuck in this
thing day and night, in a house full of ramps. And to
add insult to serious injury – I've totally given up
smoking, my favourite thing, and the truth is . . .
we can't have a baby.

Dead silence.

William   Belle.

Bella shrugs her shoulders. Bernie is totally grief-struck.

Bernie   No. Not true . . .

Bella   C'est la vie . . . We're lucky in lots of ways, but . . .
Surely it's worth a brownie.

William reaches for her hand. Max breaks the
sombre mood.

Max   Well, I don't know. Look at William. Very unsuccessful
       professionally. Divorced. Used to be handsome, now
       kind of squidgy round the edges – and absolutely
       certain never to hear from Anna again after she's heard
       that his nickname at school was Floppy.

They all laugh. Anna smiles across at William.

William So I get the brownie?

Max   I think you do, yes.

Anna   Wait a minute. What about me?

Max   I'm sorry? You think you deserve the brownie?

Anna   Well . . . a shot at it.

William You'll have to prove it. This is a great brownie and I'm
       going to fight for it. State your claim.

Anna   Well, I've been on a diet since I was nineteen, which
       means basically I've been hungry for a decade. I've had
       a sequence of not nice boyfriends – one of whom hit
       me: and every time my heart gets broken it gets
       splashed across the newspapers as entertainment.
       Meantime, it cost millions to get me looking like this . . .

Honey Really?

Anna   Really – and one day, not long from now . . .

       While she says this, quiet settles round the table. The thing
       is – she sort of means it and is opening up to them.

       . . . my looks will go, they'll find out I can't act and
       I'll become a sad middle-aged woman who looks a bit
       like someone who was famous for a while.

       Silence . . . they all look at her . . . then.

Max   Nah!!!! Nice try, gorgeous – but you don't fool anyone.

       The mood is instantly broken. They all laugh.

William Pathetic effort to hog the brownie.

49. **int. Max and Bella's Kitchen/Living Room/ Corridor. Night.**

Anna and William are leaving.

Anna   That was such a great evening.

Max   I'm delighted.

He holds out his hand to shake. She kisses him on the cheek. He stumbles back with joy.

Anna   And may I say that's a gorgeous tie.

Max   Now you're lying.

Anna   You're right. I told you I was bad at acting.

Max loves this.

Anna   *(to Bella)* Lovely to meet you.

Bella   And you. I'll wait till you've gone before I tell him you're a vegetarian.

Max   No!

Anna   Night, night, Honey.

Honey   I'm so sorry about the loo thing. I meant to leave but I just . . . look, ring me if you need someone to go shopping with. I know lots of nice, cheap places . . . not that money necessarily . . . *(gives up)* nice to meet you.

And Honey gives her a huge hug.

Anna   You too – from now on you are my style guru.

Anna and William head out . . . Bernie tries to save some dignity.

Bernie   Love your work.

They move to the door and wave goodbye.

50.   ext. Max and Bella's House. Night.

William and Anna step outside. From inside they hear a massive and hysterical scream of the friends letting out their true feelings. William is a little embarrassed.

William   Sorry – they always do that when I leave the house.

The house is in Lansdowne Road, on the edge of Notting Hill. They walk for a moment. A bit of silence.

Anna   Floppy, huh?

William   It's the hair! It's to do with the hair.

Anna   Why is she in a wheelchair?

William   It was an accident – about eighteen months ago.

Anna   And the pregnancy thing – is that to do with the accident?

William   You know, I'm not sure. I don't think they'd tried for kids before, as fate would have it.

They walk in silence for a moment. Then . . .

Would you like to come . . . my house is just . . . ?

She smiles and shakes her head.

Anna   Too complicated.

William   That's fine.

Anna   Busy tomorrow?

William   I thought you were leaving.

Anna   I was.

51.   ext. Notting Hill Garden. Night.

A little later in the walk.

Anna   What's in there?

They are now walking by a five foot railing, with foliage behind it.

William	Gardens. All these streets round here have these mysterious communal gardens in the middle of them. They're like little villages.
Anna	Let's go in.
William	Ah no – that's the point – they're private villages – only the people who live round the edges are allowed in.
Anna	You abide by rules like that?
William	Ahm . . .

Her look makes it clear that she is waiting with interest on the answer to this.

Heck no – other people do – but not me – I just do what I want.

He rattles the gate, then starts his climb – but doesn't quite make it, and falls back onto the pavement . . .

(casually) Whoopsidaisies.

Anna	What did you say?
William	Nothing.
Anna	Yes you did.
William	No I didn't.
Anna	You said 'whoopsidaisies'.

Tiny pause.

William	I don't think so. No-one says 'whoopsidaisies', do they – I mean unless they're . . .
Anna	There's no 'unless'. No-one has said 'whoopsidaisies' for fifty years and even then it was only little girls with blonde ringlets.
William	Exactly. Here we go again.

He fails, and unfortunately, spontaneously . . .

Whoopsidaisies.

They look at each other.

It's a disease I've got – it's a clinical thing. I'm taking pills and having injections – it won't last long.

Anna	Step aside.
	She starts to climb.
William	Actually be careful Anna – it's harder than it looks . . .
	But she's already almost over.
	Oh no it's not – it's easy.
	A few seconds later. Anna jumps down into the garden.
Anna	Come on, Flops.
	William clambers over with terrible difficulty, dusts himself off, and heads towards where she stands.
William	Now seriously – what in the world in this garden could make that ordeal worthwhile?
	She leans forward – and, for the first time since the first time – she kisses him. This time a proper kiss. A tiny pause.
	Nice garden.

52. **ext. Magic Garden. Night.**

They walk around the garden. It's a moonlit dream.
We see the lights of the houses that surround the garden.
They come across a single, simple wooden bench.

Anna   'For June, who loved this garden – from Joseph who
always sat beside her.'

We cut in and see an inscription carved into the wood.
She doesn't read the dates, carved below – 'June Wetherby,
1917 – 1992.' She is slightly choked by it.

Some people do spend their whole lives together.

He nods. They are standing on either side of the bench,
looking at each other. The camera glides away from them,
up into the night sky, leaving them alone in the garden.
Music plays.

53.   int. William's Living Room. Evening.

William in a towel rushes downstairs, having just had a shower. He shoots past Spike.

William   Bollocks, bollocks, bollocks. Have you seen my glasses?

Spike   No 'fraid not.

William   Bollocks. *(still searching – with no help from Spike)* This happens every time I go to the cinema. Average day, my glasses are everywhere – everywhere I look, glasses. But the moment I need them they disappear. It's one of life's real cruelties.

Spike   That's compared to, like, earthquakes in the Far East or testicular cancer?

William   Oh shit, is that the time? I have to go.

54.   int. William's Living Room/Corridor. Evening.

He sprints downstairs, now fully dressed.

William   *(not meaning it)* Thanks for your help on the glasses thing.

Spike   *(sincerely)* You're welcome. Did you find them?

William   Sort of.

55.   int. Cinema. Night.

Mid-film. We move across the audience. And there in the middle of it, we see Anna, watching the screen, and next to her, William, watching the film keenly, through his scuba-diving goggles.

56.   int. Restaurant. Night.

A very smart Japanese restaurant. We see Anna and William sitting, near the end of their meal.

Anna   So who left who?

William   She left me.

Anna   Why?

William	She saw through me.
Anna	Uh-oh. That's not good.

We've been aware of the conversation at a nearby table — now we can hear it. Two slightly rowdy men.

Lawrence	No – No – No! Give me Anna Scott any day.

William and Anna look at each other.

Gerald	I didn't like that last film of hers. Fast asleep from the moment the lights went down.

Again – Anna reacts.

Lawrence	Don't really care what the films are like. Any film with her in it – fine by me.
Gerald	No – not my type at all really. I prefer that other one – blonde – sweet looking – has an orgasm every time you take her out for a cup of coffee.

Anna mouths 'Meg Ryan'.

Lawrence	Meg Ryan.

William and Anna smile – they're enjoying it.

Gerald	Drug-induced, I hear – I believe she's actually in rehab as we speak.

Lawrence	Whatever, she's so clearly up for it.
	Anna's twinkle fades.
	You know – some girls, they're all 'stay away chum' but Anna, she's absolutely gagging for it. Do you know that in over fifty percent of languages the word for 'actress' is the same as the word for 'prostitute'.
	This is horrible.
	And Anna is your definitive actress – someone really filthy you can just flip over . . .
William	Right, that's it.
	He gets up and goes round the corner to the men. There are in fact four of them, the two meeker men, Gavin and Harry, hanging on the other guys' witty words.
	I'm sorry to disturb you guys but –
Lawrence	Can I help you?
William	Well, yes, I wish I hadn't overheard your conversation – but I did and I just think, you know . . .
	He's not a very convincing or frightening figure.
	. . . the person you're talking about is a real person and I think she probably deserves a little bit more consideration, rather than having jerks like you drooling over her . . .
Lawrence	Oh sod off, mate. What are you, her dad?
	Anna suddenly appears at his side and whips him away without being recognised.
William	I'm sorry.
Anna	No, that's fine. I love that you tried . . . time was I'd have done the same.
	They walk on and then . . .
	In fact – give me a second.
	And she walks straight back to their table.
	Hi.

	There's something slightly awry. He doesn't notice.
William	Hi.
	He kisses her gently on the cheek.
	To be able to do that is such a wonderful thing.
Anna	*(pause)* You've got to go.
William	Why?
Anna	Because my boyfriend, who I thought was in America, is in fact in the next room.
William	Your boyfriend?
	He is duly shocked. She's trying to be calm.
Anna	Yes . . .
Jeff *(v/o)*	Who is it?
	Jeff drifts into view behind. He is a very famous film star and looks the part – well built, very handsome. Unshaven, he has magic charm, whatever he says. Over a t-shirt, he wears a shirt, which he unbuttons as he talks.
William	Ahm . . . room service.
Jeff	How you doing? I thought you guys all wore those penguin coats.
William	Well, yes – usually – I'd just changed to go home – but I thought I'd just deal with this final call.
Jeff	Oh great. Could you do me a favour and try to get us some really cold water up here?
William	I'll see what I can do.
Jeff	Still, not sparkling.
William	Absolutely. Ice cold still water.
Jeff	Unless it's illegal in the UK to serve liquids below room temperature: I don't want you going to jail just to satisfy my whims . . .
William	No, I'm sure it'll be fine.
Jeff	And maybe you could just adios the dishes and empty the trash.

William	Right.
	And he does just that. Scoops up the two used plates and heads to the bin.
Anna	Really – don't do that – I'm sure this is not his job.
Jeff	I'm sorry. Is this a problem?
William	Ah – no. It's fine.
Jeff	What's your name?
William	Ahm . . . Bernie.
	Jeff slips him a fiver.
Jeff	Thank you, Bernie. *(to Anna)* Hey – nice surprise, or nasty surprise?
Anna	Nice surprise.
	He kisses her.
Jeff	Liar. *(to William)* She hates surprises. What are you ordering?
Anna	I haven't decided.
Jeff	Well, don't over-do it. I don't want people saying, 'There goes that famous actor with the big, fat girlfriend.'
	He wanders off taking off his t-shirt.
William	I better leave.
	Anna just nods.
	– this is a fairly strange reality to be faced with. To be honest, I didn't realise . . .
Anna	I'm so sorry . . . I don't know what to say.
William	I think goodbye is traditional.

59. int. Ritz Corridor. Night.

William walks away.

60. **ext. Ritz. Night.**

William walks down the arcade outside the hotel. He is stunned.

61. **ext. London Bus. Night.**

William sits alone on a bus. We see him through the side window. As it drives away, we see that the whole back of the bus is taken up with a huge picture of Anna.

62. int. William's Bedroom. Night.

He goes into his room and sits on the bed.

63. int. Spaceship. Night.

Space Anna, in the very hi-tech environment and a serious mood, fastens the last clasps on her uniform. She takes a helmet type thing, and places it on her head.

64. int. Coronet Cinema. Night.

Cut round to the Coronet cinema where this film is showing. It's not full. The camera moves and finds, sitting on his own . . . William. Just watching. We see a momentous flash of light from the screen explode, reflected in his eye.

65.   int. William's Living Room. Evening.

William is looking out the window, lost in thought.
Spike enters.

Spike   Come on – open up – this is me – Spikey – I'm in
contact with some quite important spiritual vibrations.
What's wrong?

Spike settles on the arm of a chair. William decides to
open up a bit . . .

William   Well, okay. There's this girl . . .

Spike   Aha! I'd been getting a female vibe. Good. Speak on,
dear friend.

William   She's someone I just can't – someone who . . .
self-evidently can't be mine – and it's as if I've taken
love-heroin – and now I can't ever have it again. I've
opened Pandora's box. And there's trouble inside.

Spike nods thoughtfully.

Spike   Yeh. Yeh . . . tricky . . . tricky . . . I knew a girl at
school called Pandora . . . never got to see her
box though.

He roars with laughter. William smiles.

William   Thanks. Yes – very helpful.

66.   int. Tony's Restaurant. Night.

Only two tables are being used. William and his friends
are on their first course. Bernie reads an 'Evening
Standard', with a picture of Anna and Jeff at
Heathrow Airport.

Max   You didn't know she had a boyfriend?

William   No – did you?

Their looks make it obvious that everyone did.

Bloody hell. I can't believe it – my whole life ruined
because I don't read 'Hello' magazine.

Max	Let's face facts. This was always a no-go situation. Anna's a goddess and you know what happens to mortals who get involved with the gods.

William	Buggered?

Max	Every time. But don't despair – I think I have the solution to your problems.

William	Really?

They all look to him for wise words.

Max	Her name is Tessa and she works in the contracts department. The hair, I admit, is unfashionably frizzy – but she's as bright as a button and kisses like a nymphomaniac on death row. Apparently.

67.   int. Max and Bella's Kitchen/Living Room. Night.

The kitchen. William is looking uneasy. A doorbell rings.

Max	Now – try.

William nods. Max heads off to the door. We stay with William – and just hear the door open and a voice come down the corridor.

Tessa (v/o)	I got completely lost – it's real difficult isn't it? Everything's got the word 'Kensington' in it – Kensington Park Road, Kensington Gardens, Kensington bloody Park Gardens . . .

They reach the kitchen. Tessa is a lush girl with huge hair.

Max	Tessa – this is Bella my wife.

Tessa	Oh hello, you're in a wheelchair.

Bella	That's right.
Max	And this is William.
Tessa	Hello William. Max has told me everything about you.
William	*(frightened)* Has he?
Max	Wine?
Tessa	Oh yes please. Come on, Willie, let's get sloshed.

She turns to take the wine and William has a split second to send a message of panic to Bella. She agrees – it's bad.

68. **int. Max and Bella's Kitchen/Conservatory. Night.**

Max walks over to the table. Honey, Bella, William and another girl.

Max	Keziah – some woodcock?
Keziah	No, thank you – I'm a fruitarian.
Max	I didn't realise that.

It is left to William, who has been set up here, to fill the pause.

William	And ahm – what's a fruitarian exactly?
Keziah	We believe that fruits and vegetables have feelings so we think cooking is cruel. We only eat things that have actually fallen from the tree or bush – that are, in fact, dead already.
William	Right. Right. Interesting stuff. *(pause)* So these carrots . . .

Keziah　Have been murdered, yes.

William　Murdered? Poor carrots. How beastly.

69.　**int. Max and Bella's Conservatory. Night.**

Time for coffee and chocolates. Beside William sits the final, perfect girl. She is Rosie, quite young, smartly dressed, open-hearted. It is just Max and William and Bella and her.

Rosie　Delicious coffee.

Max　Thank you. I'm sorry about the lamb.

Rosie　No – I thought it was really, you know, interesting.

William　Interesting means inedible.

Rosie　Really inedible – yes that's right.

They all laugh. It's going very well.

70.　**int. Max and Bella's Corridor. Night.**

William is with Rosie by the door – just about to say goodbye.

Rosie　Maybe we'll meet again some time.

William　Yes. That would be . . . great.

She kisses him gently on the cheek. He opens the door – she walks out. He shuts the door quietly and heads back into the living room . . .

71.   **int. Max and Bella's Living Room. Night.**

Max and Bella wait excitedly.

Max   Well?

William   She's perfect, perfect.

Bella   And?

William makes a gentle, exasperated gesture, then . . .

William   I think you have forgotten . . . *(he looks at them)* . . . what an unusual situation you have here – to find someone you actually love, who'll love you – the chances are . . . always miniscule. Look at me – not counting the American – I've only loved two girls in my whole life, both total disasters.

Max   That's not fair.

William   No really, one of them marries me and then leaves me quicker than you can say Indiana Jones – and the other, who seriously ought to have known better, casually marries my best friend.

Bella   *(pause)* Still loves you though.

William   In a depressingly asexual way.

Bella   *(pause)* I never fancied you much actually . . .

They all roar with laughter.

I mean I loved you – you were terribly funny. But all that kissing my ears . . .

William   Oh no – this is just getting worse. I am going to find myself, 30 years from now, still on this couch.

Bella   Do you want to stay?

William   Why not – all that awaits me at home is a
masturbating Welshman.

Music starts to play to take us through these silent scenes.

72.   **int. Max and Bella's Living Room. Night.**

Max lifts Bella off her couch and carries her upstairs.

*Mix through – William sits on the couch downstairs –
eyes wide open – thinking.*

73.   **int. Max and Bella's Kitchen/Living Room. Day.**

*Morning. Max, all in his suit for the city . . . Bella kisses
him goodbye. William sees this from the kitchen. She is
also dressed for work – and moves back into the kitchen to
pack her briefcase with law books from the kitchen table.*

74.   **ext. Max and Bella's House. Day.**

*William emerges from the house, a little ruffled from a
night away from home, and heads off.*

75. ext. Newsagent. Day.

William walks past the newsagent, heading for home.
We see, though he doesn't, a rack of tabloid papers, all of
which seem to have very grainy, grabbed pictures of Anna
on their front page. Headlines – 'Anna Stunna' – 'It's
Definitely Her!' and 'Scott of Pantartica'.

76. **int. William's Bathroom. Day.**

William is shaving. The bell goes. He heads out to answer it.

77. **ext./int. William's House. Day.**

William arrives at the door and opens it. There stands a dark-glassed Anna.

Anna Hi. Can I come in?

William Come in.

She moves inside. Her hair is a mess – her eyes are tired. Nothing idealised.

78. **int. Living Room. Day.**

The two of them.

Anna They were taken years ago – I know it was . . . well, I was poor and it happens a lot – that's not an excuse –

but to make things worse, it now appears someone was filming me as well. So what was a stupid photo-shoot now looks like a porn film. And well . . . the pictures have been sold and they're everywhere.

William shakes his head.

I didn't know where to go. The hotel is surrounded.

William   This is the place.

Anna   Thank you. I'm just in London for two days – but, with your papers, it's the worst place to be.

She's very shaken.

These are such horrible pictures. They're so grainy . . . they make me look like . . .

William   Don't think about it. We'll sort it out. Now what would you like – tea . . . bath . . . ?

Anna   A bath would be great . . .

79.   **int. William's Corridor. Day.**

Spike enters through the front door. William doesn't hear him. Spike is reading the newspaper with the Anna pictures in it.

Spike   Christ alive . . . brilliant . . . fantastic . . . magnificent . . .

He heads up the stairs. Opens the bathroom door, walks in.

80.   **int. William's Bathroom. Day.**

Spike heads for the toilet – undoes his zip . . .

Anna   You must be Spike.

She's in the bath. Spike turns in shock – and sidles out of the bathroom.

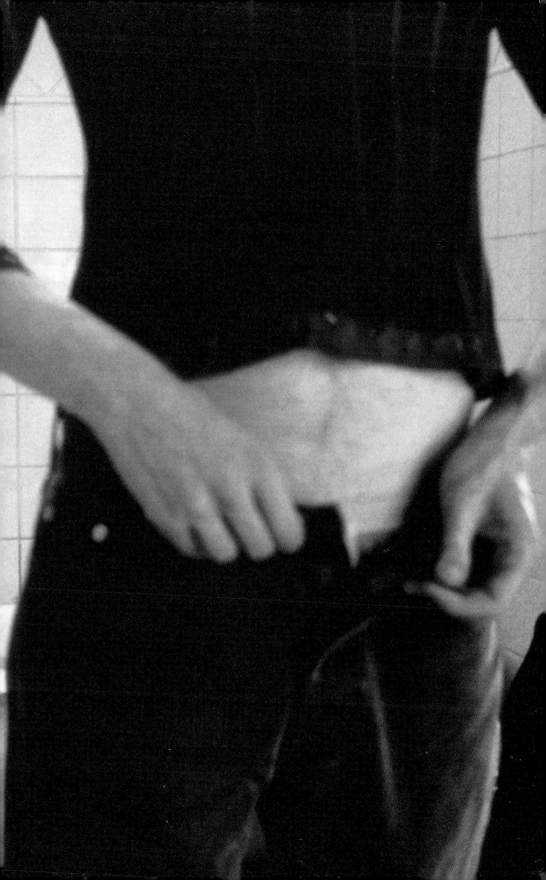

81. int. William's Corridor. Day.

Spike calms himself down. He then opens the bathroom door again – and looks in.

82. int. William's Bathroom. Day.

Anna is still lying low in the bath.

Anna   Hi.

Spike   Just checking.

83. int. Corridor. Day.

Spike comes back out into the corridor. Looks to heaven.

Spike   Thank you, God.

84. **int. William's Kitchen. Day.**

William and Anna at the kitchen table, eating toast, drinking tea.

Anna   I'm really sorry about last time. He just flew in – I had no idea – in fact, I had no idea if he'd ever fly in again.

William   No, that's fine. It's not often one has the opportunity to adios the plates of a major Hollywood star. It was a thrill for me. *(she smiles. Pause)* How is he?

Anna   I don't know. It got to the point where I couldn't remember any of the reasons I loved him. And you . . . and love?

William   Well, there's a question – without an interesting answer.

Anna   I have thought about you.

William   Oh no no – no.

He doesn't think she has to talk about this.

Anna   Just anytime I've tried to keep things normal with anyone normal – it's been a disaster.

William   I appreciate that absolutely. *(changing subject tactfully)* Is that the film you're doing?

Anna   Yes – start in L.A. on Tuesday.

William   Would you like me to take you through your lines?

Anna   Would you? It's all talk, talk, talk.

William   Hand it over. Basic plot?

Anna   I'm a difficult but brilliant junior officer who in about twenty minutes will save the world from nuclear disaster.

William   Well done you.

85.	**ext. Terrace. Day.**

A little later. They're in the thick of the script.

William	'Message from command. Would you like them to send in the HKs?'
Anna	'No, turn over 4 TRS's and tell them we need radar feedback before the KFT's return at 19 hundred – then inform the Pentagon that we'll be needing black star cover from ten hundred through 12.15' – and don't you dare say one word about how many mistakes I made in that speech or I'll pelt you with olives.
William	'Very well, captain – I'll pass that on straightaway.'
Anna	'Thank you'. How many mistakes did I make?
William	Eleven.
Anna	Damn. 'And Wainwright . . . '
William	Cartwright.
Anna	'Cartwright, Wainwright, whatever your name is. I promised little Jimmy I'd be home for his birthday – could you get a message through that I may be a little late.'
William	'Certainly. And little Johnny?'
Anna	My son's name is Johnny?
William	Yup.
Anna	Well, get a message through to him too.
William	Brilliant. *(the scene's over)* Word perfect I'd say.
Anna	What do you think?
William	Gripping. It's not Jane Austen, it's not Henry James, but it's gripping.
Anna	You think I should do Henry James instead?
William	I'm sure you'd be great in Henry James. But, you know – this writer's pretty damn good too.
Anna	Yes – I mean – you never get anyone in 'Wings of a Dove' having the nerve to say 'inform the Pentagon that we need black star cover'.

William	And I think the book is the poorer for it.

Anna smiles her biggest smile of the day. He is helping.

86.   int. William's Dining Room.

Anna and William. Sat down at table. There's a picture hanging on the wall behind.

Anna	I can't believe you have that picture on your wall.

It is a poster of a Chagall painting of a floating wedding couple, with a goat as company.

William	You like Chagall?
Anna	I do. It feels like how being in love should be. Floating through a dark blue sky.
William	With a goat playing a violin.
Anna	Yes – happiness wouldn't be happiness without a violin-playing goat.

Spike enters with three pizzas.

Spike	Voila. Carnival Calypso, for the Queen of Notting Hill – pepperoni, pineapple and a little more pepperoni.
Anna	Fantastic.
William	I didn't mention that Anna's a vegetarian, did I?
Spike	*(pause)* I have some parsnip stew from last week. If I just peel the skin off, it'll be perfect.

87. **int. William's Living Room. Night.**

Later in the evening. William and Anna on their own. They're sipping coffee. A few seconds of just co-existing. Anna looks up.

Anna You've got big feet.

William Yes. Always have had.

Anna You know what they say about men with big feet?

William No. What's that?

Anna Big feet – large shoes.

He laughs.

88. **int. William's Living Room. Night.**

A few hours later – eating ice-cream out of the tub.

Anna The thing that's so irritating is that now I'm so totally fierce when it comes to nudity clauses.

William You actually have clauses in your contract about nudity?

Anna Definitely. 'You may show the dent at the top of the artist's buttocks – but neither cheek. In the event of a stunt person being used, the artist must have full consultation.'

William You have a stunt bottom?

Anna I could have a stunt bottom, yes.

William Would you be tempted to go for a slightly better bottom than your own?

Anna Definitely. This is important stuff.

William It's one hell of a job. What do you put on your passport? Profession – Mel Gibson's bottom.

Anna Actually, Mel does his own ass work. Why wouldn't he? It's delicious.

William The ice cream or Mel Gibson's bottom?

Anna Both.

89.   **int. William's Upstairs Corridor. Night.**

They are walking up the stairs – and stop at the top.

Anna   Today has been a good day. Which under the circumstances is . . . unexpected.

William   Well, thank you. *(awkward pause)* Anyway – time for bed. Or . . . sofa-bed.

Anna   Right.

Pause. She leans forward, kisses him gently, then steps into the bedroom and closes the door.

90.   **int. William's Living Room. Night.**

William downstairs – on a sofa – under a duvet. Eyes open. Thinking. Pause and pause.

He waits and waits – the ultimate 'yearn'. But nothing happens. William gets off the sofa decisively. Sits on the side of it. Then gets back in again.

Pause, pause, then . . . in the darkness, a stair creaks. There's someone there.

William   *(to himself)* Oh my God . . . *(then . . .)* Hello.

Spike	Hello. I wonder if I could have a little word.
	He drifts round the corner, half naked.
William	Spike.
Spike	I don't want to interfere, or anything . . . but she's split up from her boyfriend, that's right isn't it?
William	Maybe.
Spike	And she's in your house.
William	Yes.
Spike	And you get on very well.
William	Yes.
Spike	Well, isn't this perhaps a good opportunity to . . . slip her one?
William	Spike. For God's sake – she's in trouble – get a grip.
Spike	Right. Right. You think it's the wrong moment. Fair enough. *(pause)* Do you mind if I have a go?
William	Spike!
Spike	No – you're right.
William	I'll talk to you in the morning.
Spike	Okay – okay. Might be too late, but okay.
	Back to William thinking again. Dreamy atmosphere. And then . . . more footsteps on the stairs.
William	Oh please sod off.
Anna	Okay.
William	No! No. Wait. I . . . thought you were someone else. I thought you were Spike. I'm delighted you're not.
	The darkness of the living room. We see Anna in the shadow.

91.   **int. William's Living Room. Night.**

A few moments later. William and Anna stand in the middle of the room. He kisses her neck. Then her shoulder. What a miracle it is just to be able to touch this girl's skin. Then he looks at her face. That face. He is suddenly struck by who it is.

William   Wow.

Anna   What?

And then gets over it straight away.

William   Nothing.

And kisses her.

92. **int. William's Bedroom. Night.**

The middle of the night. They are both asleep – a yard apart. In sleep, her arm reaches out, touches his shoulder and then she wriggles across and re-settles herself, tenderly, right next to him. He is not asleep and knows how extraordinary this all is.

93. **int. William's Bedroom. Day.**

The morning.

William   It still strikes me as, well, surreal, that I'm allowed to see you naked.

Anna   You and every person in this country.

William   Oh God yes – I'm sorry.

Anna   What is it about men and nudity? Particularly breasts – how can you be so interested in them?

William   Well . . .

Anna   No seriously. I mean, they're just breasts. Every second person in the world has got them . . .

William   More than that actually, when you think about it. You know, Meatloaf has a very nice pair . . .

Anna   But . . . they're odd-looking. They're for milk. Your mum's got them. You must have seen a thousand of them – what's the fuss about?

William   *(pause)* Actually, I can't think really – let me just have a quick look . . .

He looks under the sheet at her breasts.

No, beats me.

She laughs . . .

Anna   Rita Hayworth used to say – 'they go to bed with Gilda – they wake up with me.' Do you feel that?

William   Who was Gilda?

Anna   Her most famous part – men went to bed with the dream – and they didn't like it when they woke up with the reality – do you feel that way with me?

William   *(pause)* You're lovelier this morning than you have ever been.

Anna   *(very touched)* Oh.

She looks at him carefully. Then leaps out of bed.

I'll be back.

94. **int. William's Bedroom. Morning.**

William on the bed. The door opens. It is Anna with a tray of toast and tea.

Anna   Breakfast in bed. Or lunch, or brunch.

She heads across. She smiles and sits on the bed.

Can I stay a bit longer?

William   Stay forever.

Anna   Damn, I forgot the jam.

The doorbell goes.

You get the door, I'll get the jam.

95. **int./ext. William's Corridor. Day.**

William heads down the corridor and opens the door. Outside are hundreds of paparazzi – an explosion of cameras and questions, of noise and light. The press seem to fill the entire street.

William	Jesus Christ.

He comes back inside, snapping the door behind him. Anna is in the kitchen.

Anna	What?
William	Don't ask.

She heads down the corridor, with no suspicion.

Anna	You're up to something . . .

She thinks he's fooling around. She opens the door, the same explosion. In a split second she's inside.

Anna	Oh my God. And they got a photo of you dressed like that?
William	Undressed like this, yes.
Anna	Jesus.

96.   **int. William's Kitchen. Day.**

Anna is on the phone. Spike is blithely heading downstairs to the kitchen in just his underpants.

Spike	Morning, darling ones.

He does a thumbs up to William – very excited about what he knows was a 'result'.

Anna	(*on the phone*) It's Anna. The press are here. No, there are hundreds of them. My brilliant plan was not so brilliant after all. Yeh, I know, I know. Just get me out then. (*she hangs up*) Damnit.

She heads upstairs.

William	I wouldn't go outside.
Spike	Why not?
William	Just take my word for it.

The moment William goes upstairs, Spike heads for the front door.

97. **ext. William's House. Day.**

From outside – we see this scrawny bloke in the frame of the doorway, in his grey underpants. A thousand photos. Spike poses athletically.

98. **int. William's Corridor. Day.**

Spike closes the door and wanders along to a mirror in the hallway, muttering.

Spike   How did I look?

Inspects himself.

Not bad. Not at all bad. Well-chosen briefs, I'd say. Chicks love grey. Mmmm. Nice firm buttocks.

99. **int. William's Bedroom. Day.**

William enters. He's unhappy for her. She's almost dressed.

William   How are you doing?

Anna   How do you think I'm doing?

William   I don't know what happened.

Anna   I do. Your furry friend thought he'd make a buck or two telling the papers where I was.

She's packing.

William   That's not true.

Anna	Really? The entire British press just woke up this morning and thought 'Hey – I know where Anna Scott is. She's in that house with the blue door in Notting Hill.' And then you go out in your goddamn underwear.
Spike	*(dropping in)* I went out in my goddamn underwear too.
William	Get out, Spike. *(he does)* I'm so sorry.
Anna	This is such a mess. I come to you to protect myself against more crappy gossip and now I'm landed in it all over again. For God's sake, I've got a boyfriend.
William	You do?

It's a difficult moment – defining where they stand.

Anna	As far as they're concerned I do. And now tomorrow there'll be pictures of you in every newspaper from here to Timbuktu.
William	I know, I know – but . . . just – let's stay calm . . .
Anna	You can stay calm – it's the perfect situation for you – minimum input, maximum publicity. Everyone you ever bump into will know. 'Well done you – you slept with that actress – we've seen the pictures.'
William	That's spectacularly unfair.
Anna	Who knows, it may even help business. Buy a boring book about Eygpt from the guy who screwed Anna Scott.

She heads out.

100.   **int. Stairs/Living Room. Day.**

William	Now stop. Stop. I beg you – calm down. Have a cup .of tea.
Anna	I don't want a goddamn cup of tea. I want to go home.

The doorbell goes.

William	Spike, check who that is . . . and for God's sake put some clothes on.

Spike leans merrily out of the window.

Spike	Looks like a chauffeur to me.

101. **int. William's Kitchen/Corridor. Day.**

They move from the kitchen into the corridor.

Anna   And remember – Spike owes you an expensive dinner. Or holiday – depending if he's got the brains to get the going rate on betrayal.

William   That's not true. And wait a minute . . . this is crazy behaviour. Can't we just laugh about this? Seriously – in the huge sweep of things, this stuff doesn't matter.

Spike   What he's going to say next is – there are people starving in the Sudan.

William   Well, there are. And we don't need to go anywhere near that far. My best friend slipped – she slipped downstairs, cracked her back and she's in a wheelchair for the rest of her life. All I'm asking for is a normal amount of perspective.

Anna   You're right: of course, you're right. It's just that I've dealt with this garbage for ten years now –you've had it for ten minutes. Our perspectives are different.

William   I mean – today's newspapers will be lining tomorrow's waste paper bins.

Anna   Excuse me?

William   Well, you know – it's just one day. Today's papers will all have been thrown away tomorrow.

Anna   You really don't get it. This story gets filed. Every time anyone writes anything about me – they'll dig up these photos. Newspapers last forever. I'll regret this forever.

He takes this in. That's the end.

William   Right. Fine. I will do the opposite, if it's all right by you – and always be glad you came. But you're right – you probably better go.

She looks at him. The doorbell goes again. She opens the door. Massive noise and photos. Outside are her people, including Karen, a chauffeur, two bodyguards. And then the door is shut and they're all gone. Silence.

102. **int. William's Kitchen/Corridor. Day.**

Spike and William sitting there. Pause.

William   Was it you?

Spike   I suppose I might have told one or two people down the pub.

William   Right.

He puts his head in his hands. It's over now.

103. **ext. London. Days.**

As full, sad music plays – William begins to walk through Notting Hill.

This walk takes six months . . . as he walks, the seasons actually and magically change, from summer, through autumn and winter, back into spring . . .

First it is summer – summer fruits and flowers – a six month pregnant woman – Honey with another leather-jacket boyfriend.

As he walks on the rain starts to fall – he turns up his coat collar – umbrellas appear. Followed by winter coats – chestnuts roasting – Christmas trees on sale and the first hint of snow.

Then he comes to Blenheim Crescent, which is a startling snowscape, for the hundred yards, right across Ladbroke Grove.

By the time he reaches the purple cafe, the snow is melting and in a few yards, it is spring again. He passes Honey again – arguing with her boyfriend, walking away tearful. Then turns past 'the pregnant woman' – now holding her three-month baby. The camera holds on her.

104.   **int. Bookshop. Day.**

A grey day in the bookshop. Martin and William. As ever. A feeling that things in there never change.

Ten seconds pass. Honey rushes in. Spike, still feeling in disgrace, comes in with her but lingers in the doorway.

Honey   Have we got something for you. Something which will make you love me so much you'll want to hug me every single day for the rest of my life.

William   Blimey. What's that?

Honey   The phone number of Anna Scott's agent in London and her agent in New York. You can ring her. You think about her all the time – now you can ring her!

William   Well, thanks, that's great.

Honey   It is great, isn't it. See you tonight. Hey, Marty – sexy cardy.

And she rushes out. William looks at the piece of paper, folds it and then places it gently in the garbage bin.

105. **int. Tony's Restaurant. Night.**

Bella bangs a spoon on a wine bottle. All the friends are gathered in the restaurant.

Bella   I have a little speech to make – I won't stand up because I can't . . . be bothered. Exactly a year ago today, this man here started the finest restaurant in London.

Tony   Thank you very much.

Bella   Unfortunately – no-one ever came to eat here.

Tony   A tiny hiccough.

Bella   And so we must face the fact that from next week, we have to find somewhere new to eat.

Tony's brave face breaks. The dream is over.

I just want to say to Tony – don't take it personally. The more I think about things, the more I see no rhyme or reason in life – no one knows why some things work out, and some things don't – why some of us get lucky – and some of us . . .

Bernie   . . . get fired.

Bella   No!

Bernie   Yes, they're shifting the whole outfit much more towards the trading side – and of course . . .
(he owns up) I was total crap.

They're all rather stunned.

Tony   So we go down together! A toast to Bernie – the worst stockbroker in the whole world!

They toast him.

Honey   Since it's an evening of announcements . . . I've also got one. Ahm . . . I've decided to get engaged.

Total bewilderment from the others.

I've found myself a nice, slightly odd looking bloke who I know is going to make me happy for the rest of my life.

Special cut to Bernie – the shot shows he had special feelings for Honey.

William	Wait a minute – I'm your brother and I don't know anything about this.
Max	Is it someone we know?
Honey	Yes. I will keep you informed.

As she sits down, Honey leans towards Spike and whispers.

	By the way – it's you.
Spike	Me?
Honey	Yes. What do you think?
Spike	Well, yes. Groovy.
Max	Any more announcements?
William	Yes – I feel I must apologise to everyone for my behaviour for the last six months. I have, as you know, been slightly down in the mouth.
Max	There's an understatement. There are dead people on better form.
William	But I wish to make it clear I've turned a corner and henceforward intend to be impressively happy.

106.   **int. Tony's Restaurant. Night.**

Two hours later. They've had a very good time. There's been a chocolate cake. Lots of alcohol. Tony is playing 'Blue Moon' on the piano, and Bernie joins him, singing.

At one table Bella and Honey sit – beer and wine on the table.

Bella	I'm really horribly drunk.

Elsewhere, Max and William are relaxed together.

Max	So – you've laid the ghost.
William	I believe I have.
Max	Don't give a damn about the famous girl.
William	No, don't think I do.

Max   Which means you won't be distracted by the fact that she's back in London, grasping her Oscar, and to be found filming most days on Hampstead Heath.

He puts down a copy of the 'Evening Standard' with a picture of Anna on its cover.

William   *(immediate gloom)* Oh God no.

Max   So not over her, in fact.

107.   ext. Hampstead Heath. Day.

*Cut to the wide sweep of Hampstead Heath. William
entirely alone. He marches up a hill . . . goes over the crest
of it – and sees a huge film crew and hundreds of extras in
front of the radiant white of Kenwood House, with its
lawn and its lakes.*

108. **ext. Kenwood House. Day.**

Now closer to the house, William approaches a barrier – where he is himself approached.

Security Can I help you?

William Yes – I was looking for Anna Scott . . .

Security Does she know you're coming?

William No, no. She doesn't.

Security I'm afraid I can't really let you through then, sir.

William Oh right. I mean, I am a friend – I'm not a lunatic but – no, you basically . . .

Security . . . can't let you through.

At that moment – thirty yards away, William sees a trailer door open. Out of it comes Anna – looking extraordinary – in a velvet dress; full, beautiful make-up; rich, extravagant hair. She has a necessary cluster of people about her. Hair, make-up, costume and the third assistant who has collected her.

She walks a few yards, and then casually turns her head. And sees him. Her face registers not just surprise, certainly not a simple smile. His being there is a complicated thing. Cut back to him. He does a small wave. She pauses as the whole paraphernalia of the upcoming scene passes between them. The movie divides them. But then she begins to walk through it, and followed by her cluster, she makes her way towards him. When she reaches him, the security guard stands back a pace, and her people hold back. She doesn't really know what to say . . .

Anna This is certainly . . . ah . . .

William I only found out you were here yesterday.

Anna I was going to ring . . . but . . . I didn't think you'd want to . . .

The third assistant is under pressure.

Third Anna.

She looks round. The poor third is nervous – and the first is approaching.

Anna	*(to William)* It's not going very well – and it's our last day.
William	Absolutely – you're clearly very busy.
Anna	But . . . wait . . . there are things to say.
William	Okay.
Anna	Drink tea – there's lots of tea.

She is swept away, four people touching her hair and costume.

Karen	Come and have a look . . .

109. **ext. Kenwood Park. Day.**

As they move towards the set . . .

Karen	Are you a fan of Henry James?
William	This is a Henry James film?

110. **ext. Kenwood Park. Day.**

A complicated shot is about to happen – with waves of extras – and a huge moving crane. They end up next to the sound desk.

Karen	This is Harry – he'll give you a pair of headphones so you can hear the dialogue.

Harry the sound man is a pleasant, fifty-year-old balding fellow. He hands him the headphones.

Harry	Here we go. The volume control is on the side.
William	That's great.

William, the headphones on, surveys the scene – the cluster is a full 100 yards from the action, to allow a gracious sweeping wide-shot. He watches Anna. She is with her co-star in the Henry James film – let's call him James.

James	We are living in cloudcuckooland – we'll never get this done today.

Anna	We have to. I've got to be in New York on Thursday.
James	Oh, stop showing off.

He studies an actress a few yards to the left.

God, that's an enormous arse.

Anna	I'm not listening.
James	No, but seriously – it's not fair – so many tragic young teenagers with anorexia – and that girl has an arse she could perfectly well share round with at least ten other women – and still be big-bottomed.
Anna	I said I'm not listening – and I think, looking at something that firm, you and your droopy little excuse for an 'arse' would be well-advised to keep quiet.

Back by the desk, William is listening and laughs. That's his girl. Anna prepares.

Anna	So I ask you when you're going to tell everyone, and you say . . . ?
James	'Tomorrow will be soon enough.'
Anna	And then I . . . right.
James	Who was that rather diffident chap you were talking to on the way up?
Anna	Oh . . . no-one . . . no-one. Just some . . . guy from the past. I don't know what he's doing here. Bit of an awkward situation.

111.   ext. Hampstead Heath. Day.

Cut back to William – he has heard.

William	Of course.
	He takes off the headphones and puts them gently down.
	Thank you.
Harry	Anytime.
	William walks away. The moment of hope is gone. He couldn't have had a clearer reminder.

112. **int. William's Living Room. Evening.**

William is emptying Anna Scott videos into a box.

Spike	What's going on?
William	I'm going to throw out these old videos.
Spike	No. You can't bin these. They're classics. I'm not allowing this.
William	Right – let's talk about rent . . .
Spike	Let me help. We don't want all this shit cluttering up our lives.

113. **int. Backroom of The Bookshop. Day.**

The next day. William is hard at work, doing the accounts in a dark small room with files in it. Martin pops his head in.

Martin	I hate to disturb you when you're cooking the books, but there's a delivery.
William	Martin, can't you just deal with this yourself?
Martin	But it's not for the shop. It's for you.
William	Okay. Tell me, would I have to pay a wet rag as much as I pay you?

They head out, Martin behind him, incomprehensibly rubbing his hands – he's in a very good mood.

114.   int. Bookshop. Day.

William enters – and there stands Anna – in a simple blue skirt and top.

Anna	Hi.
William	Hello.
Anna	You disappeared.
William	Yes – I'm sorry – I had to leave . . . I didn't want to disturb you.
Anna	Well . . . how have you been?
William	Fine. Everything much the same. When they change the law Spike and I will marry immediately. Whereas you . . . I've watched in wonder. Awards, glory . . .
Anna	Oh no. It's all nonsense, believe me. I had no idea how much nonsense it all was – but nonsense it all is . . . *(she's nervous)* Well, yesterday was our last day filming and so I'm just off – but I brought you this from home, and . . .

It's quite a big wrapped parcel, flat – 3 foot by 4 foot, leaning against a bookshelf.

I thought I'd give it to you.

William	Thank you. Shall I . . .
Anna	No, don't open it yet – I'll be embarrassed.
William	Okay – well, thank you. I don't know what it's for. But thank you anyway.

Anna I actually had it in my apartment in New York and just thought you'd . . . but, when it came to it, I didn't know how to call you . . . having behaved so . . . badly, twice. So it's been just sitting in the hotel. But then . . . you came, so I figured . . . the thing is . . . the thing is . . .

William What is the thing?

Then the door pings. In walks the annoying customer, Mr Smith.

William Don't even think about it. Go away immediately.

Mr Smith is taken aback and therefore completely obedient.

Mr Smith Right. Sorry.

And he leaves.

William   You were saying . . .

Anna   Yes. The thing is . . . I have to go away today but I wondered, if I didn't, whether you might let me see you a bit . . . or, a lot maybe . . . see if you could . . . like me again.

Pause as William takes this in.

William   But yesterday . . . that actor asked you who I was . . . and you just dismissed me out of hand . . . I heard – you had a microphone . . . I had headphones.

Anna   You expect me to tell the truth about my life to the most indiscreet man in England?

Martin edges up.

Martin	Excuse me – it's your mother on the phone.
William	Can you tell her I'll ring her back.
Martin	I actually tried that tack – but she said you said that before and it's been twenty-four hours, and her foot that was purple is now a sort of blackish colour . . .
William	Okay – perfect timing as ever – hold the fort for a second will you, Martin?

Martin is left with Anna.

Martin	Can I just say, I thought 'Ghost' was a wonderful film.
Anna	Is that right?
Martin	Yes . . . I've always wondered what Patrick Swayze is like in real life.
Anna	I can't say I know Patrick all that well.
Martin	Oh dear. He wasn't friendly during the filming?
Anna	Well, no – I'm sure he was friendly – to Demi Moore – who acted with him in 'Ghost'.

She's kind here, not sarcastic.

Martin	Oh right. Right. Sorry. Always been a bit of an ass.

William returns a little uneasy.

Anyway . . . it's lovely to meet you. I'm a great fan of yours. And Demi's, of course.

Martin leaves them.

William	Sorry about that.
Anna	That's fine. There's always a pause when the jury goes out to consider its verdict.

She's awaiting an answer.

William Anna. Look – I'm a fairly level-headed bloke. Not often in and out of love. But . . .

He can't really express what he feels.

. . . can I just say 'no' to your kind request and leave it at that?

Anna . . . Yes, that's fine. Of course. I . . . you know . . . of course . . . I'll just . . . be getting along then . . . nice to see you.

William The truth is . . .

He feels he must explain.

with you, I'm in real danger. It looks like a perfect situation, apart from that foul temper of yours – but my relatively inexperienced heart would, I fear, not recover if I was once again . . . cast aside, which I would absolutely expect to be. There are too many pictures of you everywhere, too many films. You'd go and I'd be . . . well, buggered, basically.

Anna I see. *(pause)* That really is a real 'no', isn't it?

William I live in Notting Hill. You live in Beverly Hills. Everyone in the world knows who you are. My mother has trouble remembering my name.

Anna Okay. Fine. Fine. Good decision.

Pause.

The fame thing isn't really real, you know. Don't forget – I'm also just a girl. Standing in front of a boy. Asking him to love her.

Pause. She kisses him on the cheek.

Bye.

Then turns and leaves. Leaving him.

115. **int. Tony's Restaurant. Day.**

The restaurant is in the middle of being deconstructed.
The pictures are gone off the walls – a kettle on a long
extension lead is on the bare table behind. They're
all sitting there.

William	What do you think? Good move?
Honey	Good move: when all is said and done, she's nothing special. I saw her taking her pants off and I definitely glimpsed some cellulite down there.
Bella	Good decision. All actresses are mad as snakes.
William	Tony – what do think?
Tony	Never met her, never want to.
William	Brilliant. Max?
Max	Absolutely. Never trust a vegetarian.
William	Great. Excellent. Thanks.
	Spike enters.
Spike	I was called and I came. What's up?
Honey	William has just turned down Anna Scott.
Spike	You daft prick!

Bella is casually looking at the painting that sits beside William. It is the original of the Chagall, the poster of which was on his wall.

Bella	This painting isn't the original, is it?
William	Yes, I think that one may be.
Bernie	But she said she wanted to go out with you?
William	Yes – sort of . . .
Bernie	That's nice.
William	What?
Bernie	Well, you know, anybody saying they want to go out with you is . . . pretty great . . . isn't it . . .
William	It was sort of sweet actually – I mean, I know she's an actress and all that, so she can deliver a line – but she said that she might be as famous as can be – but also . . . that she was just a girl, standing in front of a boy, asking him to love her.

They take in the line. It totally reverses their attitudes.
A pause.

Oh sod a dog. I've made the wrong decision, haven't I?

They look at him. Spike does a big nod.

Max, how fast is your car?

116.   **ext. Tony's Restaurant. Day.**

Max's car arrives in the street outside. They pile into
the car.

Max   If anyone gets in our way – we have small
nuclear devices.

Bernie   And we intend to use them!

Max   Where's Bella?

Honey   She's not coming.

Max   Sod that. Bernie – in the back!

He shoots out of his door, rushes round and grabs
Bella out of the chair.

Come on, babe.

117. **ext./int. Car. Stanley Crescent/Notting Hill Gate. Day.**

Max's car is shooting up Stanley Crescent. We are inside and outside the car.

Bella   Where are you going?

Max   Down Kensington Church Street, then Knightsbridge, then Hyde Park Corner.

Bella   Crazy. Go along Bayswater . . .

Honey   That's right – then Park Lane.

Bernie   Or you could go right down to Cromwell Road,
and left.

William   No!

Suddenly the car slams to a halt.

Max   Stop right there! I will decide the route. All right?

All   All right.

Max   James Bond never has to put up with this sort of shit.

118. **ext. Piccadilly. Day.**

The car turns illegally right across Piccadilly the wrong way down a one-way street and ends up outside the Ritz. William sprints into the hotel. Bernie follows.

Bernie   Bloody hell, this is fun.

119. **int. Ritz Lobby. Day.**

William   Is Miss Scott staying here?

It is the same man.

Ritz Man   No, sir.

William   How about Miss Flintstone?

Ritz Man   No, sir.

William	Or Bambi . . . or, I don't know, Beavis or Butthead?
	Man shakes his head.
Ritz Man	No, sir.
William	Right. Right. Fair enough. Thanks.
	He turns despondent and takes two steps when the Ritz Man stops him in his tracks.
Ritz Man	There was a Miss Pocahontas in room 126 – but she checked out an hour ago. I believe she's holding a press conference at The Savoy before flying to America.
	William is very grateful. He kisses the Ritz Man. Bernie's also grateful. He kisses him too.
Bernie	We have lift off !!!
	A Japanese guest assumes this is the way to behave and the Ritz Man gets kissed a third time.

120. **ext. London Streets. Day.**

The car speeds through London. It gets totally stuck at a junction where no-one will let them in.

Spike   Bugger this for a bunch of bananas.

He gets out of the car and boldly stops the traffic coming in the opposite direction. Our car shoots past him.

Go!

They leave him behind. Honey leans out the window and shouts . . .

Honey   You're my hero.

Spike waves wildly – he loses concentration and is very nearly hit by a car.

121. **ext. The Savoy. Day.**

They pull to a stop. William leaps out.

Max   Go!

122. **int. The Savoy. Day.**

William rushes up to the main desk.

William   Excuse me, where's the press conference?

Man at Savoy   Are you an accredited member of the press?

William   Yes . . .

He flashes a card.

Man at Savoy   That's a Blockbuster video membership card, sir.

William   That's right . . . I work for their in-house magazine. *(mimes quotation marks)* 'Movies are our business'.

Man at Savoy   I'm sorry, sir . . .

Honey shoots into shot, pushing Bella's chair.

Bella   He's with me.

Man at Savoy   And you are?

Bella	Writing an article about how London hotels treat people in wheelchairs.
Man at Savoy	Of course, madam. It's in the Lancaster Room. I'm afraid you're very late.
Honey	*(to William)* Run!

123.   int. Savoy Room. Day.

William runs, searching. At last finds the room, and enters.

124.   int. Lancaster Room. Day.

Huge room – full of press. Row after row of journalists, cameras at the front, TV cameras at the back. Anna clearly gives press conferences very rarely, because this one is positively presidential. She sits at a table at the end of the room, beside Karen: on her other side is Jeremy, the PR boss, firmly marshalling the questions.

Jeremy	Yes . . . You – Dominic.
Questioner 1	How much longer are you staying in the UK then?
Anna	No time at all. I fly out tonight.

She's in a slightly melancholic and therefore honest mood.

Jeremy	Which is why we have to round it up now. Final questions.

He points at a journalist he knows.

Questioner 2	Is your decision to take a year off anything to do with the rumours about Jeff and his present leading lady?
Anna	Absolutely not.
Questioner 2	Do you believe the rumours?
Anna	It's really not my business any more. Though I will say, from my experience, that rumours about Jeff . . . do tend to be true.

They love that answer, and all scribble in their note books. Next question comes from someone standing right next to William.

Questioner 3	Last time you were here, there were some fairly graphic photographs of you and a young English guy – so what happened there?
Anna	He was just a friend – I think we're still friends.
Jeremy	Yes, the gentleman in the pink shirt.

He is pointing straight at William, who has his hand up.

William	Yes – Miss Scott – are there any circumstances in which you two might be more than just friends?

Anna sees who it is asking.

Anna	I hoped there might be – but, no, I'm assured there aren't.
William	And what would you say . . .
Jeremy	No, it's just one question per person.
Anna	No, let him . . . ask away. You were saying?

William	Yes, I just wondered whether if it turned out that this . . . person . . .
Other Journalist	*(to William)* His name was Thacker.
William	Thanks. I just wondered if Mr Thacker realised he'd been a draft prick and got down on his knees and begged you to reconsider, whether you would . . . reconsider.

We cut to Max, Bella, Bernie and Honey, all watching. Then back to Anna.

Anna	Yes, I'm pretty sure I would.
William	That's very good news. The readers of 'Horse and Hound' will be absolutely delighted.

Anna whispers something to Jeremy.

Jeremy	Dominic – if you'd like to ask your question again?
Questioner 1	Yes – Anna – how long are you intending to stay here in Britain?

Pause. Anna looks up at William. He nods.

Anna	Indefinitely.

They both smile – suddenly the press gets what's going on – music – noise – they all turn and flash, flash, flash photos of William. Max and Bella kiss. Bernie kisses a total stranger. Spike finally makes it – he's bright red from running.

Spike	What happened?
Honey	It was good.

Honey hugs him. It's a new experience for Spike.

Cut to William's face – flash after flash – still looking at Anna. They are both smiling.

125.   int./ext. The Hempel Zen Garden with Marquee. Day.

Anna and William at their wedding – they kiss and walk into the crowd.

Honey, a bridesmaid in peach satin – she is surrounded by at least four other bridesmaids, all under five.

Nearby, Tony standing, glowing, beside his fabulous, pyramidical wedding cake.

William's mother is not quite happy with how he's looking. She tries to brush his hair.

Max, dressed in the most devastating Bond-like white tuxedo is dancing with Anna – thrilled. He does a rather flashy little move. Cut to Bella who is watching and laughing.

Martin, in an awkward tweed suit, is jiggling to the beat of a song, entirely happy in the corner.

126. **ext. Leicester Square. Night.**

A huge premiere – screaming crowds – Anna and William get out of the car, she holding his hand – looking ultimately gorgeous – he in a black tie that doesn't quite fit. He's startled.

127. **ext. Garden. Day.**

*A pretty green communal garden. Children are playing,
watched by mothers, one of whom holds a new baby
in a papoose. A very old couple wander along slowly.*

A small tai chi group moves mysteriously. And as the camera glides, it passes a couple sitting on a single, simple wooden bench overlooking the garden. He is reading, she is just looking out, totally relaxed, holding his hand, pregnant. It is William and Anna.

An Afterword by Hugh Grant

During the lowest ebbs of shooting 'Four Weddings and a Funeral' (the director, Mike Newell, hurling a coffee cup across a car park yelling, 'We're fucked! We're fucked!' or me having to be helped, gibbering, back onto the set after watching myself on rushes for the first time), Richard Curtis used to cheer me up by talking about the new film he was hatching, and what funny scenes he'd already thought up for me.

And in the years that followed, as I sat around flicking the pages of 'Congo II' and thinking 'maybe there is something here', the only thing that kept me from signing on the dotted line was the thought that Richard's new script was just around the corner. It never was. Never has a human being taken longer to write a perfectly straightforward romantic comedy.

Some call it perfectionism. I called it sloppy, and sent him angry faxes urging him to drop Rowan Atkinson, The Vicar of Whatsit, his own children and the world's starving and concentrate on me.

When, however – many years later – the script finally did arrive, two things scared the life out of me. One was how good it was (William Goldman: 'One of the two best screenplays of the last ten years') and the other was that Julia Roberts was going to be the girl. My nerves at the first preliminary read through in New York were out of control. Fear always goes straight to my voice and for the first twenty pages or so, whenever Julia would say something romantic and funny to me, I found I could only respond with a sort of angry bark. After that I settled down a bit and thought I was pretty funny, though Richard told me afterwards that my voice had gone incredibly high and posh, like the prep school boy in that 'Seven Up' documentary.

Rehearsals were in a freezing church hall in Notting Hill in April and went very well on the whole. The other British actors were all a bit too talented for my liking, but very nice to me. Julia was brilliant and very unstarry but so cold we had to have two men tail her around the room with gas heaters at all times to stop her passing out.

The only ugliness came when, trying to be amusing, I contrived to wrestle Gina McKee (Bella) out of her wheelchair. She was quite badly injured but charming about it.

And the shooting was great. Things I remember most clearly include –

Roger Michell, unable to get enough nicotine into his blood stream, ripping the filters off cigarettes and smoking them two at a time. (Tim McInnerny claims to have seen him behind a piece of scenery secretly experimenting with a third cigarette in one of his nostrils.)

Coming off the set after what I thought had been a particularly hilarious take and seeing Richard and Duncan Kenworthy staring at the playback monitor as though they'd both just been told they had BSE.

Julia getting me in the mood for a tricky scene by tweaking my nipples quite violently and then crushing a grape against the side of my neck.

Me doing the same to her. (Not the nipple bit.)

Rhys Ifans (Spike) having lunch in the Shepperton pub with a bunch of Welsh extras from 'The Mummy', denying he was drunk when he got back to our set, and then gleefully mouthing 'PLASTERED, MATE' to me during the actual scene.

Coming off the set after what I thought had been a rather lame take and being encouraged by all the smiles and hilarity around the playback monitor.

Finding the monitor had been tuned to England
v Colombia.

The film's brilliant make-up designer, Jenny Shircore,
telling me how great the rushes were though my
teeth were a bit yellow and my top lip non-existent.

Emma Chambers (Honey) doing a very rude and
immature thing with a chocolate brownie on my chair
during the chocolate brownies scene.

Julia and Hugh Bonneville (Bernie) swapping
embroidery designs.

Giving him a really terrible time about this.

Everyone on the streets of Notting Hill itself being
very nice to us except for one man who turned up
every day to throw eggs at us.

As to what we actually shot, I'm afraid I know
nothing. I tried a couple of times to go to rushes,
but after the 'Four Weddings' debacle (counselling,
valium) Duncan and Richard hired security men to
keep me out of the screening room.

They did recently invite some of us to see a rough
cut but I made the mistake of agreeing to meet Rhys
for a swift half beforehand, and am consequently
none the wiser.

I hope it's good, and knowing what a great job
Nicotine Man did, I'm sure it is. But even if for some
reason it isn't, I'm pretty sure – as I sit here learning
my lines for 'Congo III' – that the script is and was a
masterpiece, and I really hope you enjoyed it.

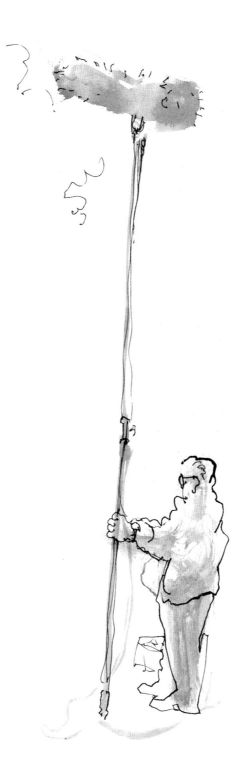

Other Bits and Other Pieces.

I started writing this film six weeks after my daughter was born, and the film is going to be released on her fourth birthday. So, you'd sort of hope there'd be some re-writes somewhere, just to fill the time. And there have been. I've put together some of the scenes that, for various reasons, went before the movie was shot – and then some others that we shot, but then perished in the pitched battle that drove this film down from the three and a half hours first cut to its still quite long two hours.

This was the original opening of the movie. It was meant to introduce all the friends and relatives. In the end, however, we decided just to concentrate on William at the beginning, and this fell by the wayside. But when Hugh and Julia accepted the film, these were the first scenes they read.

In the dark – a voice has begun . . .

William (v/o)   It was spring. My friend Tony was opening a restaurant in Notting Hill. He'd been a waiter for twenty years – and this was the day he broke free.

ext. Tony's Restaurant. Night.

The outside of the restaurant – 'Tony's Joint'. Tony welcoming guests. He radiates a simple, enthusiastic joy. There's a hugely noisy and friendly atmosphere inside. It feels like a success.

William (v/o)   It was a no-fail proposition, in the heart of Notting Hill, and all his friends were there . . .

int. Tony's Restaurant. Night.

Cut to a table of William and his group of friends. They are definitively relaxed with each other.

Max   So, you can sleep with anyone in the world – who do you choose? Bernie?

Bernie   Ahm . . . gosh . . . well, the Queen, I suppose.

William	The Queen?
Bernie	Yes. I mean, I wouldn't enjoy it or anything – but afterwards, you could say, you know, I've had the Queen – and that's got to be pretty . . . impressive.
Max	What about you, Honey?
Honey	Let's see . . .
Bernie	Actually, on second thoughts, I think maybe the Queen Mum.
Bella	Oh shut up, Bernie.
Bernie	I mean, anyone can say they've had sex with the Queen – but her mother!
Honey	I think it has to be Brad Pitt – with Mel Gibson's bottom.
William	What's wrong with Brad's bottom?
Honey	I just haven't seen it enough, that's all. Whereas Mel's always been splendidly forthcoming with his little bottie.
Max	Fair enough. Bella?
Bella	I sleep with the man I most want to sleep with every night. *(meaning Max)*
Honey	Boo!
William	Yes, that is pretty sickly.
Bella	There speaks an embittered divorcee.

We cut away to Tony for a moment, who gestures at the throbbing crowd at the bar and gives them all a huge thumbs up. His big night and it's going well.

Max	So what about you, Will? Who's your girl of girls?
William	Do you know I've never thought about it.
Honey	That's hurtful. What about me?
William	You're my sister.
Honey	Doesn't mean we don't have great sex.

Max	Be that as it may. We're talking about famous people. I'll give you twenty seconds to make up your mind.
	Meanwhile, Bernie's worried.
Bernie	*(to Honey)* That's not true about you and William and having . . . ?
Honey	Don't be silly. The odd blow job, but we'd never actually do it.
Bernie	Oh fine.
Max	So, who's it to be?
William	Seriously, there are no famous people on my list. It's all in the lighting. Up close, Cindy Crawford looks exactly like my dad.
Honey	Oh, come on, Will, this is pathetic. It is so obvious.
William	Who?
Honey	The most beautiful woman in the world, as well as my favourite actress.
Bernie	Pamela Anderson?
Bella	Bernie.
Bernie	Well, she may not be that beautiful – but she's a brilliant actress.
Max	Come on, spit it out.
Honey	Anna Scott – so clear-cut, so far in the lead.
	Pause. The camera concentrates on William.
William	Yes – well, you have a point – she is fairly fabulous . . .
Honey	She's paradise in pants. Now be honest with me – do I look anything like her – I mean anything at all like her?
	They all look at her. Pause.
Max	You both have ears.

After we'd cut that scene, this next one became the friends' first scene, fitting in after William and Anna's kiss in the corridor. We shot it – but in the end decided that it was more fun to meet them all the first time Anna meets them, at the birthday party. It also includes the first mention of Max and Bella not being able to have a baby – which, I can't deny, does rather leap out of nowhere in the film as it now stands. The price you pay.

int. Tony's Restaurant. Day.

William enters. Inside it is very full – with a bright, successful, hot feel to it. William approaches a table of friends.

William   Right – so – can you all keep a secret?

Max   Definitely.

Honey   Definitely.

Bernie   Definitely not.

Bella   Bernie!

Bernie   I hear so many things during the day, I find it impossible to remember which one was the secret one.

William	He's right. No-one can keep a secret.
Honey	This is so unfair!
William	And I was only joking anyway – as you well know, I don't have any secrets.
Max	What about that girl in Crete?
Bella	What girl in Crete?
William	There was no girl in Crete – I have never actually been to Crete.
Max	Apart from the time you went to Crete on holiday.
William	Apart from that time.
Bella	When there was apparently some incident with a girl.
William	Everyone makes one mistake in their lives.
Bernie	So is yours the one with the girl in Crete, or the business with you and that boy at school?
William	Right – change the subject – Bernie – how's work?
Bernie	Splendid thanks. Still wearing the suit and not having any idea what the hell is going on.
William	Excellent. Max, Belle – any news on the kids front? We hopeful godparents are getting seriously impatient.
Bella	Well, truth is, it's not as easy as it seems.
William	What's that?
Bella	Having children. Getting pregnant.

She's dealing here with something that is terribly serious to her.

William	I'm so sorry – I didn't know.
Bella	No, no-one knows – but . . . well I mean it's no secret, it's just that saying you're 'trying' is so . . . trying.
Max	I can't begin to describe the nightmare of it – I've spent the last three months having blood tests, shooting home at four in the afternoon for sex and masturbating into test-tubes.

Bernie	Oh dear. That's a bit rough.
Max	No matter. So . . . this secret.
William	Really it's nothing. I'll tell you when I'm very old and you'll be amazed.

Bernie's been thinking.

Bernie	Wait a minute – you actually come home at four in the afternoon and Bella lets you have sex with her?
Max	As it were.
Bernie	Bloody hell. What fabulous lives other people lead.

We shot this next scene with two wonderful actors, Ann Beach and Tenniel Evans, and in our first screening, it was the funniest scene in the film. But then with each successive screening, we started to realise it was a problem. It came after Hugh and Julia kiss in the garden and it was just slowing everything down – coming when we should only be concentrating on William and Anna falling in love. So finally we lost it. You always kill the thing you love.

int. William's Parents' Dining Room. Day.

William at lunch with his parents. There are prints of racing scenes and roses on the walls. Both parents have dressed up a bit for the lunch – father in jacket and tie – mother in a floral dress.

William	Now look – if I tell you this – you absolutely mustn't tell anyone else.
Father	Of course not.
William	Well, you say that – but this is a peculiarly strange person to have got . . . ahm . . . involved with . . .
Mother	It's not Fergie is it?

William	No, Mum – it's not Fergie.
Father	Don't want to get involved with Fergie – she'll spend all your money, make you suck her toes and then run off with the first bald man who takes her fancy.
Mother	Lady Helen Windsor is lovely.
Father	Oh yes – she's gorgeous.
William	No, you know what, strangely enough, it's not a member of the royal family at all. The truth is – and you must keep this an absolute secret – I've sort of got to know . . . Anna Scott, in fact.

They both look at him, apparently amazed. Then . . .

Mother	Who?
William	For heaven's sake – you know her – we watched that film of hers on telly last Christmas – come on . . .
Father	Anna Scott. Oh yes. That's right. Splendid. *(pause)* And how are things at the bookstore?
William	No, stop – we can't end the conversation there. Try to take this in, Dad – it's like the equivalent in your generation of you going out with Vivien Leigh, or Grace Kelly.
Mother	Poor Grace.
William	What do you mean, 'Poor Grace'?
Mother	What a terrible way to die. Those poor children.
William	I'm not talking about how she died – I'm talking about how incredible it would have been to kiss her when she was alive.
Father	I remember the first time I kissed your mother . . .
Mother	Now, be careful here, darling.
Father	It was a boiling hot day . . .
William	No, we're drifting again . . . remember, we were talking about me and Anna Scott.

Mother	I do remember her now. She's that pretty girl, isn't she. Looks a bit like Mavis.
Father	Dear Mavis – she and Gerald have had such a difficult year. Arthritis is such a bugger.
Mother	Poor things.
William	Yes. Right. Good . . . (totally resigned to failure here) How's Deidre? Still teaching?

While I was writing the film, I went out for lunch in Westbourne Grove, where I bumped into a friend of mine called Alec, a director. He was having lunch with Gwyneth Paltrow – and although we talked for three minutes, he never introduced us. Quite rightly – I had very big hair that week, and no-one wants to be thought of as a friend of someone who looks like a mixture between Cilla Black and Margaret Thatcher. When I got back to the office, I wrote this scene. It nearly made it in, just before the Whoopsidaisies scene.

ext. West End Streets. Night.

William and Anna are walking along together. A pleasant tension. They pass a laughing couple – a little drunk – in love. Then . . .

Anna	Oh God – a weird-looking guy's coming straight at us. You're in charge.

She puts on her glasses.

Friend	Hi. William?

The suspected madman comes through the darkness, William recognises him. It's a friend.

William	Yes – hey, how you doing?
Friend	Great, fine, good to see you.

Anna relaxes, since it's a friend – takes off her glasses and does a little semi-apologetic wave and smile. The friend smiles back.

William	Well, everything trucking along, as usual?
Friend	Not exactly – since I lost the job things have been pretty hard – but I'm sort of getting back my equilibrium.
William	Oh great. Well – yes, I was sad about all that – but I'm really pleased it's all coming right. You're looking well, anyway.
Friend	Hair's different but . . .
William	Yeh, the hair really is something. Well, great to see you.
Friend	Yes – you too. Well, better be getting on.

Nods, smiling at Anna.

William	Yes, great. Take care. Bye.

The friend walks away. William drops his head in despair.

Anna	Why didn't you introduce us?
William	Because I couldn't remember his sodding name. He now thinks I'm the worst human being in the world. He thinks I didn't think he was worth introducing. He thinks I'm some bastard who dumps all his friends the first time he meets a famous person.
Anna	He can't be much of a friend, if you can't even remember his name.
William	Well, no, that's the problem – he actually is quite a good friend – I used to play football with him every week. Oh god – and he must be feeling such a total worthless turd.
Anna	Don't worry – we can fix it.

She runs after the friend.

William	What are you doing?

He runs after her. She reaches the friend. He is small and balding slightly.

Anna	Hi – William didn't introduce us – my name's Anna.

Hugo	Hi – yes – I know – I'm Hugo.

William catches up.

Anna	He knows I'm a bit cautious about strangers – but I mean, obviously, I didn't mean him not to let me meet a good friend like you . . . Hugo.

Tiny register on William's face – 'that's the name!'.

Anna	Old footballing friends I hear.
Hugo	Yep, every week. Donkey in goal, me on the wing.
Anna	I never knew 'Donkey' was such an athlete. Anyway – won't hold you up. Just wanted to say 'hello', and, you know . . .

She gives him a peck on the cheek.

Oh God – I'm all confused now – stick with Donkey – or simply walk away with the mysterious stranger in tweeds the touch of whose cheek has stolen my fickle heart.

Hugo is totally thrilled

Hugo	Well, I think you better stick with him. I'm . . . married actually. But . . . it's very nice to meet you. And maybe we can team up again soon, eh, Donko?
William	Absolutely – Hugo my man.
Hugo	Catch you round.
Anna	Bye.

He walks away with a high spring in his step. There is a moment of things feeling right. They head on.

Anna	Donkey, huh?
William	I don't know where that name came from. No logical explanation was ever given to me for how that came to be my nickname.

She laughs.

This was almost the first scene I wrote for the movie, even though it came very near the end of the plot, and it was my favourite scene. We shot it – the actors acted their socks off – and yet somehow in the edit it seemed superfluous. The problem was, it came after 'Ain't No Sunshine' and, in terms of woe, the song had done the job already.

int. Bookshop. Day.

A grey day in the bookshop. Martin and William. Time hangs heavy.

William	Martino.
Martin	Capo di capo.
William	Question.
Martin	Do my best.
William	In your experience of love . . .
Martin	Yes . . .
William	What credence do you give to the concept of time the healer?
Martin	Right. *(thinks about it, then . . .)* Well, when I was at college, I fell in love with a girl who wasn't interested in me at all. For three years – not interested at all. I haven't seen her since.
William	How long's that?
Martin	Seven years.

He fiddles about in his back pocket and finds his wallet. Leafs through it – takes out an old black and white picture, which he unfolds. It is a dark-haired girl, smiling, and wearing a university scarf.

I look at it every day. No-one else has ever made a mark.

William nods.

William	I thought as much.

Another scene that came in the falling-in-love section, near the parents. I named the girl Carol after Carolyn, the first girl I seriously loved, and the first to break my heart. In a strange way, all these finding-true-love romantic comedies I've written – of which I hope this will be the last – have been an attempt to put right the awful feeling of hurt of those months after she left me. So, in terms of my writing, I owe that beautiful, sweet, mysterious dark-haired girl a lot.

ext. West End Streets. Night.

They walk, like a happy couple.

Anna   You're a big idiot.

William   Oh my God.

Anna   What?

William   That woman coming up, in the expensive coat.

Anna   What about her?

The woman, classy, well-presented, thirty-five, is approaching fast – he can't finish the sentence.

William   She was . . . my word, Carol – good to see you.

Carol   William. *(she gives him a quick kiss)* Sorry, I'm late as hell, as I am always late as hell.

William   *(already hurt again)* Oh fine, well, I won't hold you up. Anna – this is Carol. We were . . . married for years. Carol – Anna.

Anna   Hello.

Carol   Hi.

Very casual – then she realises who it is. She slowly looks across at William and then back at Anna. She can't quite keep her mouth closed.

Hi.

William   You're looking lovely.

Carol	Oh no – the hair's a disaster. George hates it and says he can't look at me.
Anna	Tell him he's wrong.
Carol	I will. I will.

She runs out of steam. She can't take her eyes off her ex-husband's date.

William	How's little George?
Carol	As horrible as big George.
William	That *is* horrible. Well, you're late as hell – you better be running on. It would be lovely if you rang sometime. I'm where I was. Where we were.
Carol	I will ring. *(to Anna)* Nice to meet you.

She walks away – banjaxed by Anna. William also seems shaken.

Anna	Are you okay?
William	Yes. Yeh. It's just . . .

A big smile.

If you have to bump into your ex-wife for the first time in four years – what a fantastic person to be with when it happens.

Anna	God, you're shallow.
William	I know.

We watch them as they walk away.

And profoundly ashamed of it.

Three more yards – and then he does a big skip into the air – total glee.

This is another scene we shot, which was pretty well the heart of the film. But once again – as so often happens – looks, music, rhythms tell the story in a completely unexpected way, and things that seemed crucial become superfluous. Also, it was meant to come before the scene on Hampstead Heath – and somehow there was a feeling that it was time for William himself to take decisive action, rather than having to be pushed into it by his friends. It's a pity, because Tim was wonderful in this scene.

ext. Portobello Road. Night.

Cut to after dinner. Max and William are strolling along Portobello. They pass Woolworths window, showing posters of stars, including Claudia Schiffer and Cindy Crawford.

Max   Are you a Claudia or a Cindy man?

William   Cindy, I think.

Max   Yes, I'm Cindy too. Clauds is perfection – but she has got to be punished for the whole David Copperfield thing.

They stroll along.

Just incidentally – and I'm only saying this for your own good – you know what an absolute bloody nightmare this stuff with Bella has been.

This catches William off his guard.

William   Of course.

Max   I mean I love us not talking about it. If you talked about it, we'd both smack you. But it's a real pain in the arse. The muscles in her legs are just . . . she has to do this electric stimulation thing. Kate Moss is the one I really adore . . .

William   I agree. Nice local girl.

Max   And she has had to have so much love for me not to have spent the last year shouting at me because I make so many bloody mistakes and had to go back to work too quickly and get panicky when she smokes and anyway . . . the reason I mention it is . . . I'm getting a nagging suspicion that of all disasters you actually fell in love with your American girl.

William looks across at him.

And if it is a love thing – well then: whatever the price – you have to pay it.

William   Meaning?

Max   Meaning, you have to go to that film set and tell that bloody enormous movie star that you're absolutely the man for her and she'd be stark staring mad not to spend the rest of her life with you . . . and your very attractive friends.

William   Ha. And she'll say – 'get out of the way of the camera, you dismal pasty-faced nonentity.'

Max   Maybe. The risk of total failure is, of course, part of the price of love.

They keep walking.

William   Hmmm. *(a few strides. Then . . .)* Hampstead Heath, you say.

Max   Paper says tomorrow's the final day.

William   Classic.

Penultimately, a fourth girlfriend, exquisitely played by Sally Phillips, from the sequence where William is force-dated. She turned out to be a girlfriend too far.

int. Max and Bella's Kitchen/Conservatory. Night.

Cut back to Max at the stove.

Max   Right – prepare for the pudding . . .

He opens the steaming door and takes out something very burnt . . .

which I think is ice-cream on its own.

He walks over to the table: Bernie, Honey, Bella, William – it's a week later and there's another girl, Bernie's choice.

Max   Ice-cream, Caroline?

Caroline Oh absolutely, pile it on.

Huge grin on Bernie's face. She's doing well. She's a very cheerful, quite posh type. In that green jumper.

William   And tell me, Caroline – what do you do?

Caroline Sorry – not with you . . .

William   What do you do – as a job?

Caroline Oh gotcha, right. Yes. Absolutely. Sorry. Durr. Ah, no, right. Ahm. No. I teach actually.

William   Oh. Right. What age?

Caroline I'm 28, come June.

William   Right. And how old are the children you teach?

Caroline Oh God – is that what you meant? Sorry. Had my brains just scooped out with a great big spoon. Ahm – no – sorry – ahm – what was the question?

William   How old are the children you teach?

Caroline	Actually they're not children. They're dogs. And they come in all ages.
William	Classic. Challenging stuff.

The final scene here is just to show how far a film can travel. In the first draft I wrote, the character of Honey was not William's sister – she worked in the record store opposite his bookshop and actually went out with him after Anna the movie star slipped out of his life. The original movie was about a man choosing between someone sweet and poor who wore glasses and the most glamorous woman in the world. And he chose Honey. But in the end, I just couldn't bear to dismiss either of them, so I made Honey a sister and sorted things out with Anna instead. This is a scene where the original Honey finally decides to stand up for herself. William has just gone swimming to try to sort out his horrible dilemma.

int. Porchester Baths. Day.

We see William swimming away – 10 lengths, 20 lengths, 30 lengths. Thinking.

Finally he makes his way into the men's locker-room – and is having a shower.

Naked man	You did a lot of lengths.
William	Yes, well, I've got a lot to think about.
Naked man	Right.

He comes out. And in walks Honey.

Honey	Hi.
William	Honey.
Honey	I've been thinking.
William	So have I. I'll be changed in a minute – I'll come out.
Honey	No, I'm keen to talk about it now.
William	The thing is, women aren't actually allowed . . .
Honey	Oh don't be such a drip.

The naked man appears and is startled by her being there – he rushes off to find a towel – and then has a lot of trouble over the next two minutes trying not to let her see him naked again – he doesn't seem to have enough hands to open his locker and get things out without his towel slipping off – and in the end – the towel comes right down, when he's turned her way. But that is in the background – we're half watching that – and half watching Honey talking to William.

You clearly have a decision to make of some sort – and I just want to say something about that. The thing is . . . don't just judge me by what I am, Willie . . .

William   I'm not judging anyone . . .

Honey   Judge me by . . . what I'd like to be. I may just be a girl in a record store – but in my heart, I'm all the girls whose records I sell – I'm Barbra Streisand and Edith Piaf, I'm Chrissie Hynde and Janis Joplin, I'm crazy Sinead and sensible Bonnie Raitt and stupid Cyndi Lauper. I'm Madonna and I'm Ella Fitzgerald. I'm more than I seem. I'm all the things I dream.

William   Sweetheart.

Honey   And I love you, which is another thing.

William takes this in.

Well, that's it. I'll leave you now.

William   No, stay – I'll be out in a minute.

Honey   No, I think you have all the facts. I look forward to your decision.

Honey turns to the troubled naked man.

And in case you're worried, or curious, yes, that is a very small penis indeed.

And she leaves . . .

It is, as you can see, a long, long road, with many a winding turn.

Cast List

In order of appearance

William Thacker	Hugh Grant	*Loud men in restaurant*	Dorian Lough
Tony	Richard McCabe		Sanjeev Bhaskar
Spike	Rhys Ifans		Paul Chahidi
Martin	James Dreyfus		Matthew Whittle
Anna Scott	Julia Roberts	*Tessa*	Melissa Wilson
Rufus the Thief	Dylan Moran	*Keziah*	Emma Bernard
Annoying Customer	Roger Frost	*Perfect Girl*	Emily Mortimer
Ritz Concierge	Henry Goodman	*Security Man*	Tony Armatrading
'Time Out' journalist	Julian Rhind-Tutt	*3rd Assistant Director*	September Buckley
Anna's Publicist	Lorelei King	*Harry the Sound Man*	Philip Manikum
PR Chief	John Shrapnel	*Anna's co-star*	Sam West
'Helix' Lead Actor	Clarke Peters	*Japanese Businessman*	Dennis Matsuki
Foreign Actor	Arturo Venegas	*Savoy Concierge*	Patrick Barlow
Interpreter	Yolanda Vasquez	*Journalists*	Andy de la Tour
10 Year Old Actress	Mischa Barton		Maureen Hibbert
Max	Tim McInnerny		Rupert Proctor
Bella	Gina McKee		David Sternberg
Honey	Emma Chambers	*William's Mother*	Ann Beach
Bernie	Hugh Bonneville		

Unit List

Casting by	Mary Selway
Original Music	Trevor Jones
Production Designer	Stuart Craig
Costume Designer	Shuna Harwood
Editor	Nick Moore
Director of Photography	Michael Coulter BSC
Executive Producers	Tim Bevan
	Richard Curtis
	Eric Fellner
Written by	Richard Curtis
Produced by	Duncan Kenworthy
Directed by	Roger Michell
Line Producer	Mary Richards
1st Assistant Director	Chris Newman
Camera Operator	Mike Roberts
Script Editor	Emma Freud
Hair & Make-up Design	Jenny Shircore
Sound Recordist	David Stephenson
Supervising Art Director	John King
Set Decorator	Stephenie McMillan
Location Manager	Sue Quinn
Wardrobe Supervisor	John Scott
Financial Controller	Michele Tandy
Post-production Supervisor	Deborah Harding
Supervising Sound Editor	Ian Fuller
Construction Co-ordinator	Michael Redding
Executive in Charge of Production	Jane Frazer
Focus Puller	John Jordan
Clapper Loader	Tim Battersby
Grip	Colin Manning
Camera Trainee	Joe Gormley
Video Operator	Sue Harper
Script Supervisor	Libbie Barr
Sound Maintenance	Charlie McFadden
Sound Assistant	John Lewis
Playback Operator	Mike Harris
Second Assistant Director	Bernard Bellew
Co-second Assistant Director	Ben Howarth
Crowd Assistant Director	Sue Wood
Floor Runner	Emma Horton
FT2 Trainee	
Third Assistant Director	Charlie Hayward
Production Co-ordinator	Simon Fraser
Production Assistant	Karen McLuskey
Production Runner	Jon Brown
Assistants to Duncan Kenworthy	Francesca Castellano
	Wendy Dade
Assistant to Roger Michell	Tiane Wilson
Assistants to Richard Curtis	Sally Ann Ritchie
	Sarah McDougall
	Belinda Curtis
Assistant to Eric Fellner	Lara Thompson
Assistant to Tim Bevan	Juliette Dow
Assistant to Julia Roberts	Suzanne Weinert
Assistant to Hugh Grant	Sara Woodhatch
For Working Title Films	
Senior Vice President of Business Affairs	Angela Morrison
Vice President of Business Affairs	Rachel Holroyd
Marketing Co-ordinator	Amelia Granger
Director of Finance	Julian Tomlin
Legal Assistant	Çigdem Worthington
Company Co-ordinator	Nina Khoshaba
Production Accountant	Betty Williams
Assistant Accountant	Rajeshree Patel
Accounts Assistant	Jean Simmons
Accounts Trainee	Claire Robertson
Post-production Accountant	Brian Bailey
Location Unit Managers	Michael Harm
	Jeremy Johns
Location Assistant	Joseph Jayawardena
Casting Assistant	Jennifer Duffy
US casting Consultants	David Rubin, Ronna Kress,
	Debra Zane
Product Placement Consultants	Lynette Jackson and
	Kellie Robson of I.E.M. Ltd
Unit Publicist	Patric Scott
Stills Photographer	Clive Coote
First Assistant Editor	Gabrielle Smith
Lightworks Assistant Editors	Ben Yeates, Stephen Boucher,
	Liz Roe
Optical Supervisor	Peter Dansie
Music Editor	Peter Clarke
Second Assistant Editor	Andrew Perrier
Editing Trainee	Lea Morement
NFTS Trainees	Nicholas Chaudeurge
	Young-mi Lee
Work Experience	Andrew Haigh
Dialogue Editor	Philip Alton
Effects Editor	Derek Lomas
Foley Editors	Nigel Mills
	Grahame Peters
Assistant Sound Editor	Ian Macbeth
Julia Roberts' Make-up Designed by	Richard Dean
Julia Roberts' Hair Designed by	Lyndell Quiyou
Hugh Grant's Hairdresser	David Fields
Hair & Make-up Artists	Norma Webb
	Lizzie Yianni Georgiou
Hair & Make-up Trainee	Mai Layton
Wardrobe Mistress	Jane Petrie
Costumer for Julia Roberts	Francisca Vega-Buck
Wardrobe Assistants	John Denison
	Claire Smith
Costume Design Assistant	Kay Manasseh
Additional Wardrobe Assistants	Barbara Brady
	Anthony Brookman
	Nigel Egerton
	Lester Mills
	Natalie Ward
	Alison Wyldeck
Art Directors	Andrew Ackland-Snow
	David Allday
Assistant Set Decorator	Miraphora Mina
Production Buyers	Brian Read
	Deborah Stokely
Draughtsmen	Alan Gilmore
	Peter Dorme
Junior Draughtsman	Al Bullock
Food Stylist	Christine Greaves
Art Department Assistant	Alexandra Walker
Translights by	Alan White, Stilled Movie Ltd
Scenic Artist	Brian Bishop
Assistant Scenic Artist	Doug Bishop
Graphic Artist	Robert Walker
Property Master	Barry Wilkinson
Prop Storeman	Stan Cook
Chargehand Dressing Propman	Bernie Hearn
Dressing Propmen	Peter Wallis
	Jamie Wilkinson
	Sydney Wilson
Chargehand Standby Propman	Simon Wilkinson
Standby Propmen	Ben Wilkinson
	Gary Ixer
Construction Buyer	Richard Lyon
H.O.D. Carpenter	Ken Pattenden
Supervising Carpenters	Geoff Ball
	George Coussins
	Keith Dyett
	Paul Jones

Carpenters	Dominic Ackland-Snow
	John Burn
	Steven Corke
	Richard Denyer
	Paul Hayes
	Freddie Myatt
	Ray Norris
	Keith Pitt
	Frederick Round
	Nicola Russo
	Norman Simpson
	Bryan Smith
	Daniel Thompson
	Alan Tilley
	David Trice
	David Williamson
Chargehand Wood Machinist	Richard Rowlands
Wood Machinist	Ronald Nicholls
H.O.D. Painter	Kavin Hall
Supervising Painter	Peter Western
Chargehand Painter	Robert Hill
Painters	Ernie Bell
	Bob Harper
	Martin Hedinger
	Peter Mounsey
	Lee Shelley
	David Skinner
Chargehand Painters Labourer	Paul Budd
Trainee Painter	Richard Hall
Supervising Rigger	Peter Wallace
Chargehand Rigger	Ian Pape
Riggers	Tony Cardenas
	Andy Challis
	David Price
Supervising Stagehand	Ken Wilson
Chargehand Stagehand	Terry Newvell
Stagehands	Mark Bailey
	Malcolm Carlo
	Len Serpant
	Clive Wheeler
Master Plasterer	Don Taylor
Supervising Plasterer	Neil Clark
Plasterers	David Baynham
	Tony Boxall
	Allan Croucher
	Ian McFadyen
	Brian Pegg
	Andy Sandbach
	Roy Seers
	Keith Shannon
	Anthony Turner
Chargehand Plasterer's Assistant	Otis Bell
Plasterer's Labourers	Ashley Bell
	Brian Cooper
	Gordon O'Reilly
Standby Carpenter	Stephen Eels
Standby Painter	Ray Campbell
Standby Rigger	Ian Rolfe
Standby Stagehand	Christopher Hedges
Gaffer	Terry Edland
Best Boy	Tony Hayes
Electricians	Kevin Edland
	Darren Gattrell
	Paul Kemp
	Ricky Pattenden
Generator Operator	Mark Laidlaw
Rigging Gaffer	Wayne Leach
Rigging Electricians	Tom O'Sullivan
	Mark Evans
	Dave Ridout
	Sam Bloor
	Terry Townsend
Electrical Rigger	Richard Law
Practical Electrician	Eric Melville

Additional Camerawork	
Translight and Insert Cameraman	Stefan Lange
Camera Operator	Chris Plevin
Steadicam Operator	Peter Robertson
Documentary Cameraman	Michael Eley
16mm Camera Operator	Paul Otter
Wescam Operator	John Murzano
Wescam Assistant	Steve North
Visual Effects Supervisor	Tim Webber
Digital Visual Effects	CFC & FrameStore
Digital Visual Effects Producers	Fiona Walkinshaw
	Sharon Lark
Digital Visual Effects Designers	Dan Glass
	Paddy Eason
	Pedro Sabrosa
Paint Artist	Alex Payman
Titles Designed by	Chris Allies
Music Recorded & Mixed by	Simon Rhodes and Gareth Cousins
	at Abbey Road Studios, London
Performed by	The London Symphony Orchestra
Leader	Janice Graham
Conducted by	Geoffrey Alexander
Synthesizers Performed by	Trevor Jones
Synthesizers Recorded	
and Mixed by	Gareth Cousins at CMMP Studio
Orchestrations	Trevor Jones, Geoffrey Alexander,
	Julian Kershaw
Electric Guitars Arranged	
and Performed by	Clem Clempson
Piano Performed by	Dave Arch
Acoustic Guitar Performed by	Craig Ogden
Music Co-ordination for CMMP	Victoria Seale
Executive in Charge of	
Music for PFE	Dawn Solér
Soundtrack Co-ordinators	Marc Marot
	Nick Angel
Health & Safety Officer	Paul Jackson
Unit Nurse	Jeanie Udall
Construction Nurse	Teresa Johnson
Choreographer	Geraldine Stephenson
Stunt Co-ordinator	Nick Gillard
Additional Production Assistants	Jane Burgess, John Fensom,
	Phil Hill, Nathan Holmes,
	Toby Hosking, Dan Leon,
	Cian O'Leary, Fiona Richards,
	Sarah Robinson, Nick Simmonds,
	Andrea Slater, Phil Stoole,
	Dathi Sveinbjarnarson,
	Lee Taylor, Tracey Tucker
EPK Crew	Paul Sommers, Anthony Palmer,
	John Sorapure, Dave Williams.
Stand-ins	Steve Ricard, Viviane Horne,
	David Field, Joan Field,
	Debbie Hanney, Paul Kite
Unit Drivers	Mike Beavan
	Tommy Lee
	Enyo Mortty
	Terry Reece
	John Smith
Facility Truck Drivers	Neal Pierson, John Ott,
	Dennis Swan, Mike Harris,
	Scott Henley, Chas Hughes,
	Dave Jones, Albert Smith,
	Peter Newson, Bill Turner,
	Mick Boddy, Gerry Batson,
	Steve Pike, Howard Doubtfire,
	Mike Moran, Rob Todd
Unit Security	Ismahil Blagrove, Jason Moyce,
	Ray Grey, Darren Stock,
	Roy Stock, Ricky Stupple,
	Dale Williams, Tony Ambrose,
	Steve Fisher, Mitch King,
	Steve Lemaitre, Malcolm Perkins

Security for Julia Roberts
Provided by   SISS Ltd

Post-production Consultancy by   Steeple Post Production
Services Ltd
Re-recording Mixers   Robin O'Donoghue and
Dominic Lester
Assisted by   Richard Street
ADR/Foley Mixer   Ed Coyler
Assisted by   David Tyler

ADR Voice Casting   Louis Elman
Foley Artists   Pauline Griffiths
Paula Boram

Insurance Services Supplied by   Near North Entertainment Ltd
Camera and Lenses by   Movietech Camera Rentals Ltd
Cranes & Grip Equipment
Supplied by   Arri Media Grip
Lighting Equipment Supplied by   Lee Lighting Ltd
Editing Equipment Supplied by   London Editing Machines,
Edithire, Salon

Originated on Motion Picture
Film from   Kodak
Color by   Deluxe
Negative Cutting   Sylvia Wheeler Film Services Ltd
Colour Timer   Clive Noakes
Film Opticals   General Screen Enterprises
Colour Dupes   Film & Photo Ltd
Sound re-recorded at   Shepperton Sound,
Shepperton Studios, England
Post-production Facilities   De Lane Lea Ltd
Stills Processing   Pinewood Stills
Video Transfer   Telefilm Video Services, TVI Ltd,
Midnight Transfer
Post-production Scripts   Sapex Scripts
Footage Licensing   Karen Dola
Legal Services Provided by   Frank Bloom of Marriott Harrison

Extras Casting   Sue Wood
Crowd Casting Agencies   20/20 Productions Limited
Ray Knight
Costumiers   Angels & Bermans
Cosprop Ltd
Moss Bros.
Wigs Made & Supplied by   Terry Jarvis
Horses & Carriages   Debbie Kaye
Greenery   Filmscapes Ltd
Special Effects Rain   Effects Associates Ltd
Special Effects Snow   Snow Business
Flowers by   Moyses Stevens Ltd

Transport/Facility Vehicles
Supplied by   Lays International Ltd
Location Facilities Ltd
Film Flow Ltd
Studio Workshop

Catering Services   Set Meals Ltd
Caterers   Paul Caldicott
Rebecca Wiseman
Maree 'Digger' Glen
Sophie Hutchins

Acknowledgements   'La Mariée' by Marc Chagall
© ADAGP.
Paris & DACS, London 1998.

'Cossacks' by Wassily Kandinsky
© ADAGP.
Paris & DACS, London 1998.
Print supplied by
Tate Gallery, London.

Footage courtesy of
Entertainment Tonight and
Paramount Pictures Corporation

Special Thanks to   The Ritz Hotel
The Savoy Hotel
The Hempel
Nobu Restaurant
The Metropolitan Hotel
UCI Cinemas for the
Empire Leicester Square
English Heritage and
Kenwood House, Hampstead
The Royal Borough of Kensington
& Chelsea
City of Westminster Council
Notting Hill Police Station
West End Central Police Station
Charing Cross Police Station
and
Everyone in Notting Hill

Filmed on location in Notting Hill, London and at Shepperton
Studios and Ealing Studios, London, England.

**They were a wonderful crew. Due to them it
was a very happy shoot. Everything you see
in the film is their work.**